the Three Cornered World

Natsume Soseki

the Three Cornered World

TRANSLATED BY ALAN TURNEY

Gateway Editions
Washington, D.C.

UNESCO Collection of Representative Works: Japanese Series
This book has been accepted in the Japanese Translations Series of the United Nations Educational, Scientific, and Cultural Organization (UNESCO).

Gateway Editions™ is a trademark and Regnery® is a registered trademark of Salem Communications Holding Corporation.

ISBN: 978-0-89526-768-9
eISBN: 978-1-68451-376-5

Library of Congress Control Number: 67-28480

Published in the United States by
Gateway Editions
An Imprint of Regnery Publishing
A Division of Salem Media Group
Washington, D.C.

Manufactured in the United States of America

2022 Printing

Books are available in quantity for promotional or premium use. For information on discounts and terms, please visit our website: www.Regnery.com.

"An artist is a person who lives in the triangle which remains after the angle which we may call common sense has been removed from this four-cornered world."

SOSEKI

INTRODUCTION

I

Natsume Kinnosuke, better known by his pen-name of Soseki, was born in Tokyo in 1867, one year before the Meiji Restoration which marked the beginning of the influx of Western thought and literature into Japan. The early part of his education was concerned largely with the Chinese classics. This set him apart from many of the other writers of the period who went to mission schools, and thus came under a strong Western influence.

In 1884 he went to the Yoshimon College intending to become an architect. Later, however, he changed his mind and entered the department of literature of Tokyo Imperial University from which he graduated in 1892. While at university, he formed a close friendship with Masaoka Shiki who was the greatest name in the revival of Haiku (Hokku) poetry at that period. This friendship undoubtedly exercised a profound influence on his writing, for although he is principally famous as a novelist, the Haiku with which he often intersperses his prose are a mark of the essentially Japanese quality of his work, and are of great literary merit. After finishing a post-graduate course in 1895, Soseki became a middle school teacher, and then went on to teach at high school.

In 1896 he was married, and four years later was sent to London by the Japanese Ministry of Education to study English literature. The experience he gained here, added to his knowledge of the Chinese classics, gave him a breadth of background unique among his contemporaries. Moreover, it enabled him to form a balanced view of the comparative merits of Western and Oriental literature, and saved him from the blind hero-worship of all things foreign that was detrimental to the work of many Japanese writers of the time.

After three years in England, Soseki returned to Japan and was appointed lecturer in English literature in Tokyo Imperial University. It was about this time that his *London Letters,* published in a magazine edited by Masaoka, first began to attract attention. As yet, however, he had received no real acclaim as a writer. In 1905 he published his first novel *Wagahai wa Neko de aru (I am a Cat),* and immediately rose to fame. During the next ten years, there followed a whole stream of works both long and short, including *Botchan, Kusa Makura* and *Kokoro (The Heart of Things).* With the publication of each new work, his position as the foremost literary figure in Japan became more and more firmly established. Like Tennyson during the Victorian era in England, he became the acknowledged voice of the age. Although unlike Tennyson, who was in essential agreement with his fellow Victorians, Soseki more often than not indulged in ruthless criticism of his contemporary society. It is, therefore, all the more remarkable that he became so popular in his own lifetime, considering that his was the role of critic, and not of one who sang the praises of the newly emerging 'modern' (meaning Westernised) age. The probable reason for his popularity was that it was realised that his criticisms were constructive, and based upon a patriotic desire not to see Japan sacrifice her great and long tradition in favour of the indiscriminate adoption of Western culture.

Soon after Soseki wrote *I am a Cat,* he resigned from the

university for financial reasons, and took a job as literary editor of the Asahi newspaper. In 1910 he contracted ulceration of the stomach, and it was this that caused his premature death at the age of 49 in 1916.

II

With the coming of the Meiji era, a large amount of Western literature found its way into Japan. Not only were many works translated, but many authors adopted Western brands of philosophy, and in general followed the European concepts of literature. The schools of the novel which existed in Europe began to appear in Japan too.

Soseki saw the dangers of such undiscerning copying, and realised that no worthwhile works would be produced as long as Japanese writers merely tried to repeat formulae that were entirely alien to them. He himself succeeded in creating a happy blend between the new imported ideas and the traditions of Japanese literature. Thus he, more than any other writer, provides a bridge between Japanese classical and present-day literature. It has been said that Soseki was anti-Western, but I think it is truer to say that he was pro-Japanese in an age when it was fashionable to revere everything foreign. It is the very Japanese quality of his work that has made him a lasting favourite among his fellow countrymen.

Soseki's achievement in becoming and remaining the greatest figure in modern Japanese Literature appears all the more impressive when one realises that only one other author, Mori Ogai, took an independant stand, and that every other major writer belonged to some school or another. Some say that Soseki created his own school, but while undoubtedly he eventually gained a large following in the literary world, the whole of his writing was aimed at destroying schools and advocating a greater freedom of approach.

III

Kusa Makura literally means *The Grass Pillow,* and is the standard phrase used in Japanese poetry to signify a journey. Since a literal translation of this title would give none of the connotations of the original to English readers, I thought it better to take a phrase from the body of the text which I believe expresses the point of the book.

In this, more than in any of his other more conventional novels, Soseki shows his opposition to the Realist, Naturalist and Romantic schools that were flourishing around him. Soseki has been accused of taking a God-like view of humanity because he considers himself superior to his fellow men. This, however, is not so. There is, of course, a great deal in the world to which he does consider himself superior. This is what he terms the vulgar or common world, and which he believes is unworthy of his attention as an artist. He feels that it is the artist's job to portray beauty, and that he must transcend the vulgar in order to do so. When, however, he refers to rising above human relationships and emotions, it is not that he despises them, but that he feels he must stand back and view them objectively in order to see them in their proper perspective.

Soseki's apparent desire to get away from the world and immerse himself in Nature may at first sight seem Wordsworthian. There is, however, a vast difference between Wordsworth's and Soseki's view of Nature. To Wordsworth, Nature was a reflection of God the creator. To Soseki, it was not the reflection of anything, but was one facet of essential beauty.

Soseki's method of describing both Nature and his other physical surroundings is that of the painter. Every scene he presents is in perfect proportion, as though he were reproducing it on canvas. He also makes detailed allusion to colours, shapes and textures. Indeed, so graphic is his description, that a certain Japanese artist, having read *Kusa Makura*, actually painted the scenes which appear in it. One's first impression of *Kusa Makura* is that it is a series of essays illustrated by the author with verbal sketches. This, however, is a superficial view, for in fact just the opposite is true. It is the illustrations that come first, and the so-called essay passages which follow from them. When Heinrich Heine wrote his *Harze Reise,* he was merely using his journey as a vehicle for conveying his ideas on life. With Soseki, however, what he sees about him is of primary importance, and it is some object in his surroundings which provides the stimulus for one of his philosophical flights.

From *Kusa Makura* we are able to get a clearer insight into the mind of the author than from any of his other novels. There is no need to wonder whether such-and-such a character is meant to represent Soseki or not, for here we have his thoughts and opinions set out plainly for all to see. If it is true that one can come to know a people through its literature, then I believe that *Kusa Makura* tells us more about the Japanese than any other book written since the beginning of the Meiji era.

Alan Turney
Tokyo, August 1964

✦ 1 ✦

Going up a mountain track, I fell to thinking.

Approach everything rationally, and you become harsh. Pole along in the stream of emotions, and you will be swept away by the current. Give free rein to your desires, and you become uncomfortably confined. It is not a very agreeable place to live, this world of ours.

When the unpleasantness increases, you want to draw yourself up to some place where life is easier. It is just at the point when you first realise that life will be no more agreeable no matter what heights you may attain, that a poem may be given birth, or a picture created.

The creation of this world is the work of neither god nor devil, but of the ordinary people around us; those who live opposite, and those next door, drifting here and there about their daily business. You may think this world created by ordinary people a horrible place in which to live, but where else is there? Even if there is somewhere else to go, it can only be a 'non-human' realm, and who knows but that such a world may not be even more hateful than this?

There is no escape from this world. If, therefore, you find life hard, there is nothing to be done but settle yourself as comfortably as you can during the unpleasant times, although you may only succeed in this for short periods, and thus make life's brief span bearable. It is here that the vocation of the artist comes into being, and here that the painter receives his divine commission. Thank heaven for all those who in devious ways by their art, bring tranquillity to the world, and enrich men's hearts.

Strip off from the world all those cares and worries which make it an unpleasant place in which to live, and picture before you instead a world of graciousness. You now have music, a painting, or poetry, or sculpture. I would go farther, and say that it is not even necessary to make this vision a reality. Merely conjure up the image before your eyes, and poetry will burst into life and songs pour forth. Before even committing your thoughts to paper, you will feel the crystal tinkling, as of a tiny bell, well up within you; and the whole range of colours will of their own accord, and in all their brilliance, imprint themselves on your mind's eye, though your canvas stands on its easel, as yet untouched by the brush. It is enough that you are able to take this view of life, and see this decadent, sullied and vulgar world purified and beautiful in the camera of your innermost soul. Even the poet whose thoughts have never found expression in a single verse, or the painter who possesses no colours, and has never painted so much as a single square foot of canvas, can obtain salvation, and be delivered from earthly desires and passions. They can enter at will a world of undefiled purity, and throwing off the yoke of avarice and self interest, are able to build up a peerless and unequalled universe. Thus in all this, they are happier than the rich and famous; than any lord or prince that ever lived; happier indeed than all those on whom this vulgar world lavishes her affections.

After twenty years of life I realised that this is a world worth living in. At twenty five I saw that, just as light and darkness are but opposite sides of the same thing, so wherever the sunlight falls it must of necessity cast a shadow. Today, at thirty my thoughts are these: In the depths of joy dwells sorrow, and the greater the happiness the greater the pain. Try to tear joy and sorrow apart, and you lose your hold on life. Try to cast them to one side, and the world crumbles. Money is important, but be that as it may, when it accumulates does it not become a worry which attacks you even in sleep? Love is a delight; yet should the delights of love, piling one upon another, begin to bear down on you, then you will yearn for those days long ago before you knew them. It is the shoulders of the state, the Cabinet, which are supporting the burden for the millions, its feet; and the onus of government weighs heavily upon them. Refrain from eating something particularly tasty, and you will feel you have missed something. Eat just a little, and you will leave the table with your appetite unappeased. Gorge yourself, and later you will feel uncomfortable. . . .

It was just as my meandering thoughts reached this point, that my right foot came down suddenly on the edge of a loose angular rock, and I slipped. To compensate for my left foot, which I had hastily shot out in an effort to keep my balance, the rest of me—dropped! Fortunately I came down on to a boulder about three feet across, and all that happened was that my colour-box, which I had been carrying slung from my shoulder, jerked forward from under my arm. Luckily no damage was done.

As I rose and looked around me, I noticed away off to the left of the track a towering peak shaped like an inverted bucket. It was completely covered from base to summit with dark-green foliage, but whether cryptomeria or cypress I was unable to tell.

Here and there among the greenery trail pale red patches of wild cherry in bloom, and overall hangs a haze so thick that it causes the colours to swim and blend, and makes it impossible to make out the gaps between trees and branches clearly. A little nearer is one bare mountain. It stands out sharply from its surroundings, and appears to be almost close enough to touch. Its barren flank seems to have been sheered off by the axe of some colossus, and the angular, craggy rock-face plunges fantastically, straight down to the bottom of the valley far below. That one solitary tree that I can see there on the summit is a red pine I think. Even the patches of sky showing through the branches are clearly defined. About two hundred yards farther on, my path comes to an abrupt end, but looking up I see far above a figure wrapped in a red blanket moving, down the mountain-side, and I wonder whether, if I climb, I will come out up there. This is a terrible road.

If it were only plain earth it would not take all that long, but imbedded in the ground are large stones. You can smooth the soil out flat, but the stones will stick up. You can break the stones into pieces, but not the rocks. There is nothing you can do about getting rid of the rocks. They sit atop the mound of broken earth unconquered, and with an almost contemptu-ous air of self assurance. There is nowhere here where Nature will yield us a road without a struggle. Thus, since our oppo-nent is so unaccommodating, and will not step aside, we must either climb over, or go round.

This would be no easy place to walk even if there were no rocks. As it is, the banks rise up high to left and right, and a hollow has been formed in the middle of the path. This hol-low may perhaps be best described in terms of geometry. It is a triangle of about six feet in width, whose sides shelve steeply down to meet in a sharp angle, which runs right along the centre of the track. This is more like walking along the bed of a river than along a path. Since from the very begin-ning, however, I never intended to hurry on this trip, I will take my time, and deal with the innumerable twists and turns as I come to them.

Immediately below me a lark burst suddenly into song. But gaze down into the valley as I would, I could see no sign of the bird; nor could I make out where he was singing. I could hear his voice clearly, but that was all. The ceaseless attack and vigour of his song made me feel that this vast limitless body of air was dashing backwards and forwards in a frantic effort to escape the unbearable irritation of a thousand flea-bites. That bird really did not stop even for an instant. It seemed that he would not be satisfied, unless he could sing his heart out incessantly day and night, throughout that idyllic springtime; not only sing, but go on climbing up and up for ever. There was no doubt, but that that was where the lark would die, up there among the clouds. Perhaps at the peak of his long climb, he would glide in among the drifting clouds, and there be lost for ever, with only his voice remaining, shrouded by the air.

The path swung sharply round a protruding corner of rock. A blind man would have gone headlong over the edge, but I managed, at some risk, to get past and work my way round to the right. There below me, I could see the rape-blossoms spread out like a carpet over the valley. Would a lark, I wondered, go plummeting down there?—No. Perhaps, I thought, he might come soaring up from those golden fields. Then I imagined two larks, the one diving and the other climbing, crossing each other's path in flight. It finally occurred to me that, whether diving, climbing, or crossing in flight, the vitality of the song would, in all probability, continue unabated.

In spring everything becomes drowsy. The cat forgets to chase the mouse, and men forget that they have debts. Sometimes, they even forget how to locate their own souls, and fall into a stupor. When, however, I gazed far out over that sea of rape-blossoms, I came to my senses. And when I heard the song of the lark, the mist cleared, and I found my soul again. It is not just with his throat that the lark sings, but with his whole being. Of all the creatures who can give voice to the activity of their soul, there is none so vital, so alive, as the lark. Oh, this is real happiness. When you think thus, and reach such a pitch of happiness, that is poetry.

Suddenly, Shelley's song of the lark came into my head. I tried to recite it, but I could only remember two or three verses. These are a few of the lines from those verses:

We look before and after
And pine for what is not:
Our sincerest laughter
With some pain is fraught,
Our sweetest songs are those that tell of saddest thought.

However happy the poet may be, he just cannot pour out his joys in song with the same carefree and wholehearted abandon as the lark. More obviously in Western poetry, but in Chinese poetry too, one often finds such phrases as 'countless bushels of sorrow'. It may well be that the poet's sorrow must be measured by the bushel, whereas that of the layman is not even great enough to be measured in pints. Perhaps, now I come to think about it, it is that since the poet is given to worrying more than the ordinary man, his senses have become much more acutely tuned. It is true that at times he experiences the most exquisite joy, but he also has far more than his fair share of immeasurable grief. Because of this, one should consider carefully before deciding to become a poet.

The path was level here for a short way. To the right lay a copse-covered hill, and to the left, as far as the eye could see, all was rape-blossom. Here and there I trod on dandelions, whose saw-toothed leaves stood up defiantly on all sides to defend the golden orb in the centre. I felt sorry that, being so engrossed in the sight of the rape-blossoms, I had stepped on the dandelions. However, looking back, I saw that the golden orbs were still nestling undisturbed among the protecting leaves. What a carefree existence! Once again I returned to my thoughts.

Perhaps sorrow is something which is inseparable from the poet, but when I listened to that lark singing, I felt not the slightest trace of pain or sadness; and looking at the rape-blossom I was only conscious of my heart leaping and dancing within me. The same was true with the dandelions, and the blossoming cherries, which had now passed out of sight. There in the mountains, close to the delights of Nature, everything you see and hear is a joy. It is a joy unspoiled by any real discomfort. Your legs may possibly ache, or you may feel the lack of something really good to eat, but that is all.

I wonder why this should be? I suppose the reason is that, looking at the landscape, it is as though you were looking at a picture unrolled before you, or reading a poem on a scroll. The whole area is yours, but since it is just like a painting or a poem, it never occurs to you to try and develop it, or make your fortune by running a railway line there from the city. You are free from any care or worry because you accept the fact that this scenery will help neither to fill your belly, nor add a penny to your salary, and are content to enjoy it just as scenery. This is the great charm of Nature, that it can in an instant, discipline men's hearts and minds, and removing all that is base, lead them into the pure unsullied world of poetry.

Objectively you may feel that the love of a man for his wife or his parents is beautiful, and that loyalty and patriotism are fine things. When, however, you yourself are actually involved with them, the violent flurry of pros and cons, advantages and disadvantages, will blind you to all beauty and splendour, and the poetry will be completely lost to you.

In order to appreciate the poetry, you must put yourself in the position of an onlooker, who being able to stand well back, can really see what is happening. It is only from this position that a play or novel can be enjoyed, for here you are free from personal interests. You are only a poet while you are watching or reading, and are not actually involved.

Having said this, however, I must admit that most plays and novels are so full of suffering, anger, quarrelling and crying, that even the onlooker cannot keep emotion at arm's length. He finds himself, at some point or other, drawn in, and in his turn suffers, gets annoyed, feels quarrelsome and cries. At such times, the only advantage of his position is that he is unaffected by any feeling of greed, or desire for personal gain. However, the very fact that he is disinterested means that his other emotions will be much more intense than usual. This is almost unbearable!

After thirty years of life in this world of ours, I have had more than enough of the suffering, anger, belligerence and sadness which are ever present; and I find it very trying to be subjected to repeated doses of stimulants designed to evoke these emotions when I go to the theatre, or read a novel. I want a poem which abandons the commonplace, and lifts me, at least for a short time, above the dust and grime of the workaday world; not one which rouses my passions to an even greater pitch than usual. There are no plays, however great, which are divorced from emotion, and few novels in which considerations of right and wrong play no part. The trade-mark of the majority of playwrights and novelists is their inability to take even one step out of this world. Western poets in particular take human nature as their corner stone, and so are oblivious to the existence of the realm of pure poetry. Consequently, when they reach its borders, they come to a halt, because they are unaware that anything lies beyond. They are content to deal merely in such commodities as sympathy, love, justice and freedom, all of which may be found in that transient bazaar which we call life. Even the most poetic of them is so busy dashing here and there about his daily business, that he can never even find time to forget about the next bill he will have to pay. No wonder Shelley heaved a sigh when he heard the song of the lark.

Happily, oriental poets have on occasion gained sufficient insight to enable them to enter the realm of pure poetry.

Beneath the Eastern hedge I choose a chrysanthemum,[1]
And my gaze wanders slowly to the Southern hills.

Only two lines, but reading them, one is sharply aware of how completely the poet has succeeded in breaking free from this stifling world. There is no girl next door peeping over the fence; nor is there a dear friend living far away across the hills. He is above such things. Having allowed all consideration of advantage and disadvantage, profit and loss to drain from him, he has attained a pure state of mind.

Seated alone, cloistered amidst bamboo[2]
I pluck the strings;
And from my harp
The lingering notes follow leisurely away.
Into the dim and unfrequented depths
Comes bright moonlight filtering through the leaves.

Within the space of these few short lines, a whole new world has been created. Entering this world is not at all like entering that of such popular novels as *Hototogisu*[3] and *Konjiki Yasha*.[4] It is like falling into a sound sleep, and escaping from the wearying round of steamers, trains, rights, duties, morals and etiquette.

This type of poetry, which is remote from the world and

[1] By the Chinese poet Yuan-ming.
[2] By the Chinese poet Wang Wei.
[3] & [4] Popular novels written by two of Sōseki's contemporaries. *Hototogisu* was written by Tokutomi Roka, and *Konjiki Yasha* by Ozaki Kōyō. Both novels deal with emotions and human relationships.

its cares, is as essential as sleep in helping us to stand the pace of twentieth-century life. Unfortunately, however, all the modern poets, and their readers too for that matter, are so enamoured of Western writers, that they seem unable to take a boat and drift leisurely to the realm of pure poetry. I am not really a poet by profession, so it is not my intention to preach to modern society, in the hope of obtaining converts to the kind of life led by Wang Wei and Tao Yuan-ming. Suffice it to say that, in my opinion, the inspiration to be gained from their works is a far more effective antidote to the hustle and bustle of modern living than theatricals and dance-parties. Moreover, this type of poetry appears to me to be more palatable than *Faust* or *Hamlet*. This is the sole reason why in spring I trudge all alone along mountain tracks with my colour-box and tripod slung from my shoulder. I long to absorb straight from Nature some of the atmosphere of Yuan-ming's and Wang Wei's world; and, if only for a brief period, wander at will through a land which is completely detached from feelings and emotions. This is a peculiarity of mine.

Of course, I am only human. Therefore, however dear to me this sublime detachment from the world may be, there is a limit to how much of it I can stand at any one time. I do not suppose that even Tao Yuan-ming gazed continuously at the Southern hills year in and year out. Nor can I imagine Wang Wei sleeping in his beloved bamboo grove without a mosquito net. In all probability Tao sold any chrysanthemums he did not need to a florist, and Wang made money out of the government by selling bamboo shoots to the local greengrocer. That is the sort of person I am. However much I may be enthralled by the lark and the rape blossoms, I am still mortal enough to have no desire to camp out in the middle of the mountains.

One meets other people even in a place such as this; an

old man with his kimono tucked up at the back, and a head-scarf knotted under his chin; a young girl in a red skirt; sometimes one even comes across a horse with his longer than human face. Even up here several hundred feet above sea levels surrounded by thousands of cypress trees, the air is still tainted by the smell of humanity. No, tainted is not the right word, for I am crossing this mountain in the hope of being able to spend the night in an inn at the hot-spring resort of Nakoi.

The same object may appear entirely different, just depending upon where you stand. Leonardo da Vinci once said to a pupil: 'Listen to that bell ringing. There is only one bell, but it may be heard in an infinite number of ways.'

Since our judgment of people is purely subjective, opinions about the same person, man or woman, may differ vastly. Anyway, since my object on coming on this journey was to rise above emotions, and to view things dispassionately, I am sure that people appear different to me now than they did when I lived right on top of them, in a cramped back street of that unstable and wretched city—the world of men. Even if I cannot be completely objective, then at least my feelings should be no more intense than if I were watching a Noh[1] play. At times even the Noh can be sentimental. Can anyone guarantee that he will not be moved to tears by *Shichikiòchi*[2] or *Sumidagawa*[2]? The Noh, however, is three-tenths real emotion, and seven-tenths technique. Its greatness and charm do not lie in a skillful representation of emotions and human relationships exactly as they actually are, but rather in the fact that it takes plain reality, and clothing it as it were with layer after layer of art, produces a leisurely, almost lethargic pattern of behaviour, which is to be found nowhere in real life.

[1] The Noh is very elegant classical Japanese drama, incorporating both music and dancing.
[2] Two Noh plays.

I wonder how it would be if, while I am on this short journey, I were to regard events as though they were part of the action of a Noh play, and the people I meet merely as if they were actors. Since this trip is concerned fundamentally with poetry, I should like to take the opportunity of getting near to the Noh atmosphere, by curbing my emotions as much as possible, even though I know I cannot disregard them entirely. The 'Southern hills' and the 'bamboo grove', the skylark and the rape-blossom possess a character all their own, which is vastly different from that of humanity. Nevertheless, I should like, as nearly as possible, to view people from the same standpoint as I view the world of pure poetry. Bassho[1] found even the sight of a horse urinating near his pillow elegant enough to write a Hokku[2] about. I too from now on will regard everyone I meet, farmer, tradesman, village clerk, old man and old woman alike, as no more than a component feature of the overall canvas of Nature. I know they are different from figures in a painting, since each one I suppose will act and behave as he or she sees fit. However, I think it is just plain vulgar the way the average novelist probes the whys and wherefores of his characters' behaviour, tries to see into the workings of their minds, and pries into their daily troubles. Even if the people move it will not trouble me, for I shall just think of them as moving about in a picture; and figures in a picture, however much they may move, are confined within two dimensions. If of course you allow yourself to think that they are projected into the third dimension, then complications arise, for you will find them jostling you, and once again you will be forced to consider your clash of interests. It is clearly impossible for anyone in such a situation to view things aesthetically. From

[1] Bassho Matsuo (1644–1694) is one of Japan's greatest writers. He is particularly famous for his Hokku (Haiku) poems.
[2] The Hokku (Haiku) is a poem of seventeen syllables.

23

now on I am going to observe all those I meet objectively. In this way I shall avoid any undue emotional current being generated between us, and so, however animated the other person's actions may be, they will not easily affect me. In short, it will be just like standing in front of a picture, watching painted figures rush about excitedly. Three feet away from the canvas you can look at it calmly, for there is no danger of becoming involved. To put it another way, you are not robbed of your faculties by considerations of self interest, and are therefore able to devote all your energies to observing the movements of the figures from an artistic point of view. This means that you are able to give your undivided attention to judging what is, and what is not beautiful.

It was just as I had come to this conclusion, that I glanced up and saw that the sky looked threatening. I felt as though the uncertain clouds were weighing down right on top of me. Suddenly, however, almost without my noticing, they spread out, turning the whole sky as far as I could see into a rolling, awe-inspiring sea of cloud, from which there began to fall a steady drizzle of spring rain. I had long since left the rape-blossom behind, and was now walking between two mountains. However, I was unable to tell how far away they were, for the rain was so fine, that it might have almost been taken for a mist. From time to time a gust of wind would part the high curtain of cloud, revealing off to the right a dark-grey ridge of mountain. There seemed to be a range of mountains running along there just across the valley. Immediately to my left I could see the foot of another mountain, and at times within the filmy depths of haze, shadowy shapes of what might have been pine trees showed themselves, only to hide again in an instant. Whether it was the rain or the trees that was moving, or whether the whole thing was merely the unreal wavering of a dream, I did not know. Whatever it was, it struck me as most unusual and wonderful.

The road here grew unexpectedly wide, and since it was also quite level, walking was not the back-breaking business it had been before. This was just as well, for not having come prepared for rain, I should have to hurry. The rain was just beginning to fall in drops from my hat, when, about ten or twelve yards ahead, I heard the jingling of small bells, and from out of the blackness the shape of a pack-horse driver materialized.

'I suppose you don't happen to know anywhere to stay around here, do you?'

'There's a tea-house just over a mile up the road. You've got pretty wet, haven't you?'

Still, another mile to go! I looked back, watching the pack-horse driver, like some figure on a flickering magic lantern screen, melting gradually away into the rain, until finally he disappeared completely.

The raindrops, which had before been like chaff flying in the wind, were now getting larger and longer, and I was able to see each separate shaft clearly. My haori[1] of course was saturated, and the rainwater, which had soaked right through to my underclothes, had become tepid with the heat of my body. I felt really wretched, and so pulling my hat resolutely down over one eye, I set off at a brisk pace.

When I think of it as happening to somebody else, it seems that the idea of me soaked to the skin, surrounded by countless driving streaks of silver, and moving through a vast grey expanse, would make an admirable poem. Only when I completely forget my material existence, and view myself from a purely objective standpoint, can I, as a figure in a painting, blend into the beautiful harmony of my natural surroundings. The moment, however, I feel annoyed because of the rain, or miserable because my legs are weary with walking, then I have

[1] An outer coat.

already ceased to be a character in a poem, or a figure in a painting, and I revert to the uncomprehending, insensitive man in the street I was before. I am then even blind to the elegance of the fleeting clouds; unable even to feel any bond of sympathy with a falling petal or the cry of a bird, much less appreciate the great beauty in the image of myself, completely alone, walking through the mountains in spring.

At first I had pulled my hat down over one eye and walked briskly. Later I gazed down fixedly at my feet. Finally, very subdued, I hunched my shoulders and took one dejected step after another. On all sides the wind shook the tree-tops, hurrying a solitary figure on his way. I felt that I had been carried rather too far in the direction of detachment from humanity!

✦ 2 ✦

'Anybody there?' I called, but there was no reply.

Standing under the eaves, I peeped inside. The smoke-stained and grimy shōji[1] at the back of the shop had been closed, so I was unable to see into the room which lay beyond. Five or six pairs of melancholy-looking straw sandals hanging from the sloping roof, swung listlessly to and fro. Below these stood three solitary boxes of cheap cakes, around which were scattered a few small coins.

'Anybody there?' I called again. In a corner of the earth floor inside the doorway stood a hand-mill, on which were perched a cock and a hen, their feathers puffed out in sleep. Startled by the sound of my voice, they awoke and set up an excited clucking. Just in front of the threshold there was an earthen cooking furnace, half discoloured by the rain which had been falling a little while ago. On this had been placed a tea-kettle so blackened with smoke that I was unable to tell if it was earthen or silver. I was glad to see that there was a fire in the furnace.

Again there was no answer, but nevertheless I went inside and sat down on a bench. This made the chickens beat their wings and hop from the hand-mill up on to the matted floor of the shop itself. Had it not been for the screens, they might well have gone right through into the inner room. The cock

[1] Translucent paper sliding screens.

27

crowed lustily, and to this the hen added her reedy cackling, for all the world as though they thought I were a fox or a dog. A tobacco-tray, about the size of a two-litre rice measure, had been set on a low table, and in it a coil of incense was smouldering very slowly, heedless of the passage of time. The effect of this was to give an air of tranquillity to the room. The rain was gradually easing off.

Presently I heard footsteps in the back room. Then the smoke-stained shōji slid back, and an old woman came out.

I had known all along that someone must eventually come. It was obvious with the fire alight, coins scattered around the cake boxes, and the incense smouldering leisurely. Nevertheless, this was certainly different from Tokyo if you could leave a shop wide open and unattended without any qualms. Somehow I could not quite believe that coming into a shop and sitting down on a bench uninvited, and then waiting and waiting for ages really belonged to the twentieth century. I was thoroughly enjoying this remoteness from the everyday world, but more than this, I found the old woman's face charming.

Two or three years ago I went to see *Takasago* at the Hosho Noh theatre. I remember thinking at the time that it was like looking at some beautiful painting which had been brought to life. The old man in the play, carrying a broom over his shoulder, took five or six paces along the hashigakari[1], and very slowly and sedately turning his back on the audience, came face to face with the old woman. To this day I can still see their postures as they stood there facing one another. From where I was sitting I was able to see the old woman almost full-face, and I thought how beautiful she looked. In that instant her features were indelibly imprinted on my mind. The likeness

[1] A raised passage covered with a roof, which runs obliquely through the auditorium from the dressing rooms and wings to the stage proper. It is along this that the actors make their entrances and exits.

between the old woman in the tea-shop and that image in my mind was so striking that it quite took my breath away.

'Excuse me sitting down uninvited like this, Obahsan[1].'

'Not at all. I had no idea that anyone had come in.'

'It certainly did rain, didn't it?'

'Yes, it's terrible weather. It must have been very unpleasant for you out there. Heavens, you're soaked through. I'll light a fire so you can dry yourself.'

'If you would just be kind enough to make up the furnace a little, the heat will reach me over here, and I'll soon get dry. I've got rather cold sitting here.'

'Certainly I'll make it up right away. And I'll bring you a cup of tea too.'

So saying, she stood up and shooed the chickens away. With much clucking they hopped from the grubby dark-brown matting straight down into the boxes of cheap cakes, and then flew out into the street, the cock letting his droppings fall on the cakes as he went.

'Here we are; a nice cup of tea.'

In no time at all the old woman had returned carrying a cup of tea on a shallow tray. The tea had been stewed for so long that it was almost black, but I could just make out a cluster of three plum blossoms painted roughly with one stroke of the brush on the bottom of the cup.

'Would you like a cake?'

She brought over some of the assorted cakes on which the chickens had walked. I scrutinized them carefully to make sure there were no droppings on them, but the droppings had been left behind in the box.

Over her sleeveless top-coat, the old woman tied a cord round her shoulders and under her arms to keep the sleeves of her kimono back, and squatted down by the furnace. I

[1] Obahsan literally means grandmother, but is often used to any elderly woman as a friendly or affectionate term.

took my sketch-book out from inside my kimono, and began
to draw her side-face as we talked.

'It's nice and peaceful here, isn't it?'

'Yes. As you can see it's just a small mountain village.'

'Are there any uguisu[1] here?'

'Oh yes, you can hear them singing almost every day—Even
in summer.'

'I'd love to hear them. I never get the chance, and that makes
me want to all the more.'

'It's a pity you came today. That rain a while ago has driven
them all away.'

Just then there was a crackling, and the glowing embers sent
out a sudden rush of hot air around the furnace.

'Why don't you come nearer? You must be absolutely
frozen.'

I looked up and saw the column of blue smoke break against
the eaves, and then thin out until only a few small wreathes
were left weaving themselves in and out of the rafters.

'Oh this is wonderful. Thanks to you I'm coming to life
again.'

'The weather's clearing up. Look, you can see the Tengu[2]
rock over there.'

Growing impatient with the indecision of the overcast
spring sky, the storm had resolutely swept down completely
clearing away the cloud from an angle of the mountain
which lay before us. It was at this that the old woman was
pointing. There, rising majestically into the air, was a tall
tapering rock like a pillar from which large chips have been
cut. This apparently was the Tengu rock. I gazed first at the

[1] A Japanese bird of the nightingale family.
[2] In Japanese mythology the Tengu is a goblin with a long pointed nose.

mountain, and then at the old woman. Finally, I looked half at one and half at the other, comparing them.

As an artist, I have only two impressions of old women's faces in my mind. The first is that of the old woman in *Takasago,* and the second that of the mountain witch drawn by Rosetsu. Having seen Rosetsu's picture, my conception of an old woman was as a rather weird creature; a person to be seen against a background of autumn-tinted leaves, or in a setting of cold moonlight. Thus when I saw the Noh play at the Hosho theatre, I was astonished that an old woman could have such gentle features. Unfortunately, I do not think I ever heard who carved that mask, but whoever it was, was undoubtedly an expert. Depicted in such a way even an old woman looks handsome, and has an air of gentle kindliness. Such a person would not be out of place on a gold-leafed screen, and is not at all inconsistent with the idea of soft spring breezes and cherry-blossom. At all events, as I looked at the old woman standing beside me, her arms bare, her back straight, one hand shading her eyes and the other pointing away off into the distance, I thought how much more in keeping she was with the scenery of a mountain track in springtime, than with the Tengu rock. I picked up my book and began to sketch her. Just before I had finished, however, her pose broke. Feeling rather awkward, and not quite knowing what to do with my hands, I held my book to the fire to dry.

'You look very healthy Obahsan, I must say.'

'Yes, I'm glad to say I'm still quite active. I sew, and spin hemp, and I grind the flour for the dumplings.'

I wished suddenly that I could see her turning the millstone, but since I could scarcely make such a request, I changed the subject.

'I believe it's less than two and a half miles to Nakoi from here, isn't it?'

'Yes, I would say it's just about two miles. Are you going

to the hot-spring there, sir?'

'If it isn't too crowded I may stay there. That is if I feel in the mood.'

'Well, it won't be too crowded. Since the beginning of the war[1] people have gradually stopped going there. It's just like a private house now.'

'That's wonderful. Oh, but perhaps they won't let me stay there.'

'Yes they will. You can stay there any time if you ask.'

'There's only the one inn there, isn't there?'

'Yes, just ask for Shioda, and you'll soon find it. He's the richest man in the village. In fact, it's difficult to say whether the place is really a hot-spring resort, or just his country house.'

'Well in that case, I don't suppose he minds if he never has any guests.'

'Will this be your first time at the hot-spring?'

'No, I was there once before for a while, a long time ago.'

At this point we both lapsed into silence. I picked up my book again, and was quietly sketching the chickens, when the steady jingling of horse-bells reached my ears. Indeed it penetrated them to the very depths. This jingling had a rhythm all its own, and the monotonous regularity of it beat round and round in my head. I felt just as though the hand-mill which stood next to me were lulling me into a dream with its rhythmic grinding. I stopped sketching the chickens, and wrote on the same page:

It is spring,
And the bells of packhorses invade Inen's[2] ears
Carried on the breeze.

Since I had first started up the mountain I had met five

---

[1] The Russo-Japanese war.

[2] Inen was a disciple of Basshō, who loved the tranquillity of nature.

or six horses. Every one of those five or six horses had worn trappings fitted with jingling bells! They were like creatures from some other world.

Presently, as I sat there beside the mountain path, beneath a sky already dimmed by the early evening of spring, the gentle and soothing sound of a packhorse driver's song broke through into my reverie. It was a song full of tenderness and compassion, yet somewhere locked in the depths there pulsed an irrepressible light-heartedness. I could not get it out of my head that the voice was coming from a figure in a painting. I scrawled the following lines slantwise across the page.

Swifter than the deer, a song comes on ahead through the
    spring rain.
Leaving the packhorse to follow with his tinkling bells.

When I read this poem through, however, I had the feeling that it had not been written by me at all.

'Ah, here comes someone else,' said the old woman half to herself.

Since there was only the one road, everybody, both coming and going, passed close enough to the tea-house to be seen. Each one of those five or six horses I had met recently must, with the jingling of its bells, have made the old woman think, 'Ah, here comes someone else,' only to pass on its way up or down the mountain. In that tiny village, where if you did not like flowers there was nowhere to walk, she had lived with the loneliness of the track through one spring after another. I wondered for just how long she had been living there, counting the times she heard the bells day in day out, her hair growing whiter with each succeeding year. I turned to the next page and wrote:

The songs of packhorse drivers tell the passing days,
And Spring, white hair untinted, draws on to its end.

33

But this did not express my feelings properly. It probably needed a little more planning. I sat there gazing fixedly at the point of my pencil, trying to compress into seventeen syllables[1] the ideas of white hair, a great number of years, and the songs of the packhorse drivers, in addition to the idea of spring, when the packhorse driver whose song had reached me earlier appeared in person in front of the shop, and came to a halt.

'Hello there!' he said in a loud voice.

'Why it's Gen. Are you on your way to town again?'

'Yes. If there's anything you need I'll be glad to bring it up for you.'

'Let me see. If you're going through Koji-chō, would you get me a holy tablet from the Reiganji temple for my daughter?'

'Yes, I'll get that for you. Just the one?—Your girl Aki must be happy, having married so well, eh Obasan[2]?'

'Well, she has no particular worries at the moment. Perhaps you could say she's happy.'

'Of course she's happy. Just compare her with that young lady down in Nakoi.'

'Yes, I feel really sorry for her. And she's so talented and beautiful too. Are things any better these days?'

'No, just the same.'

'Oh, what a shame,' said the old woman heaving a sigh.

'Yes, it's a shame all right,' agreed Gen stroking his horse's nose.

Clusters of raindrops still rested, after their long descent, on the leaves and blossoms among the thickly interwoven branches of the wild cherry tree outside. Just then, however, a passing gust of wind gave them a push, and unable to keep their balance, they came tumbling down in a shower from their

[1] Sōseki was writing a Hokku (Haiku).
[2] Obasan literally means aunt, but is used in the same way as Obahsan.

temporary nest. This startled the horse, and he tossed his long mane up and down. The sound of Gen's scolding voice saying, 'Whoa there;' mingled with the jingling of the horse's bells, roused me from my thoughts. The old woman was speaking.

'Gen, sometimes I still picture her now as she was on her wedding day, with her wide flowing sleeves, and her hair dressed up in a high Shimada[1] style. She was sitting on her horse, and . . . .'

'Yes that's right we didn't come by boat, we came on horse-back, didn't we Obasan?'

'Yes, and as her horse was standing under that cherry tree, some blossom fluttered down flecking her hair over which she had taken so much trouble.'

Once again I opened my sketch book. Such a scene as the old woman had described would make an excellent subject for either a picture or a poem. I could visualize her as she was on that day, and with a look of-satisfaction I wrote:

Wise is the bride who goes horseback
After the blossom has all fallen from the bough.

Strangely enough, although I had a clear impression of the clothes, the hair-style, the horse and the cherry tree, the one thing I just could not picture was the bride's face. I was searching my mind for a face that would fit, trying now one type, now another, when suddenly the face of Millais' Ophelia came to me, and slipped neatly into place beneath the high 'Shimada' hair-style. 'No, that's no good,' I thought, and immediately allowed my carefully built up picture to disintegrate. The clothes, the hair-style, the horse and the cherry tree, all completely disappeared in an instant from the scene I had created. Somewhere deep within me, however, the

[1] This is a high and very elaborate style worn particularly by brides. It somewhat resembles the style of the 'Geisha'.

misty figure of Ophelia being carried along by the stream, her hands folded in prayer, remained. It was as indestructable as a cloud of smoke which, when you beat at it with a fan, merely thins and becomes less palpable. Somehow it gave me the sort of strange and wonderful feeling as if I had been watching a long-tailed comet streaking across the sky.

'Well,' said Gen, 'if you'll excuse me I'll be on my way.'

'Call in on your way back. After that terrible downpour it must be very difficult down there along that part where the track bends so much.'

'Yes, it is rather hard going,' said Gen as he began to walk off followed by his horse.

There go those bells again.

'Does he come from Nakoi,' I asked.

'Yes, that's Gembei.'

'Who was the bride he brought on horseback through the mountain pass?'

'Shioda's daughter. He mounted her on his grey, and led her down to the town at the time of her marriage.—My, how time flies. That was, let me see, five years ago.'

Those who lament their white hair only when confronted with it in a mirror are of a happy breed, but far more of a sage was that old woman who, merely by counting the passage of five years on her fingers, could appreciate how that consuming disease, time, presses on relentlessly.

'She must have been very beautiful,' I said, 'I wish I'd been here to see her.'

'Ha, ha, ha. You can still see her now. If you stay at the hot-spring resort she's bound to come out to welcome you.'

'Is she still in the village then? It would be wonderful if she were still wearing those long billowing sleeves, and had her hair done up in a high "Shimada" style . . . .'

'Well, perhaps she'll dress up for you. Ask her and see.'

I thought this most unlikely, but was surprised to find

that the old woman was serious. This journey, on which I was trying to detach myself from emotion, would not have been very interesting had this sort of thing not occurred.

'Shioda's daughter is so much like the maid of Nagara,' continued the old woman.

'In looks, you mean?'

'Oh no, I mean the course of their lives.'

'Really? Who is this maid of Nagara?'

'Well, once upon a time, so they say, there lived in this village a girl whom men called the maid of Nagara. She was the daughter of a very rich man, and was of great beauty.'

'Go on.'

'As fate would have it, however, two men fell in love with her at the same time.'

'I see.'

'She could rest neither night nor day worrying whether to give her heart to the man called Sasada or to Sasabe. Eventually, in anguish at not being able to decide, she cast herself into the Fuchi river, and put an end to her life. Just before her death she composed this poem

From leaves of autumn flushed with love,
A pearl of dew shakes free
And falls to shatter on the earth beneath.
So too must I, to flee Love's stifling folds
Drop from the world.

I had little thought when I arrived at that small mountain village, to meet an old woman such as this, and to hear from her such a charming tale, told with such old-fashioned elegance.

'About six hundred yards down the hill, going East from here, is a five-storied pagoda quite near to the track. That's the tomb of the maid of Nagara. You should go and have a look at it on your way down to Nakoi.'

I made up my mind that I would do this.

'Shioda's daughter had the misfortune to have two men in love with her at the same time too,' said the old woman continuing her story. 'One was a man she had met while she was studying in Kyoto, and the other was the richest man in the castle town near here.'

'Really? Which one did she choose?'

'Well herself she undoubtedly wanted to marry the man in Kyoto, but for various reasons her father was against it, and made her marry the other one.'

'Well, at least she escaped having to throw herself in the river.'

'Yes, but although her husband thought her beautiful, charming and talented, and paid her every attention, somehow things did not go very well because she had been forced into the marriage in the first place. This state of affairs worried her parents very much. About this time the war broke out, and the bank for which her husband worked was ruined and had to close down. Soon after that she went back to live with her father, and since that time people have been saying what a callous, unfeeling woman she is. She used to be such a retiring, gentle girl, but lately she's become quite spirited and wild. Every time Gembei comes up here, he says how worried he is about her . . .'

I knew if I listened to any more my illusions would be spoiled. I had managed by degrees to reach an enchanted land from which I could look down on the world with complete detachment, but I felt now as though someone was demanding that I return the cloak of immortality. If, having laboriously fought every inch of the way up that steep and twisting track, I were to be foolish enough to allow myself to be dragged back down to the common everyday world, the whole point of my leaving home suddenly and wandering off like this would be lost. It is all very well to have a gossip and a chat, but you reach a point when you feel as though the smell of this wretched and unsavoury world were seeping into you through the pores of your skin, and your whole body feels heavy with dirt.

'There's just the one track leading straight the way down to Nakoi, isn't there Obahsan?' I asked standing up, and throwing a silver ten sen coin down on to the table with a clatter.

'If you turn off to the right just past the Nagara pagoda, and go down that way, it will save you about half a mile. The road's bad, but that won't worry a young man like you.—This is more than enough for the tea, thank you very much.—Mind how you go.'

✦ 3 ✦

I had a most unusual experience that first night at Shioda's. It was about eight o'clock when I arrived, and so I was unable to see what sort of house it was, or the layout of the garden. In fact it was so dark that I could not even tell which was East and which was West. I was hauled along a sort of winding corridor, and eventually shown into a small room about twelve feet by nine. This was not at all as I had remembered the place from the last time I was there. I had had my supper and a bath, and was sitting in my room drinking tea, when a young girl came in, and asked if it was all right to make the bed.

What struck me as rather odd was that the girl who had ushered me in when I had arrived, the girl who had served supper and shown me the way to the bathroom, and the girl who was now taking the trouble to make my bed for me, were all one and the same. She had, moreover, scarcely said a word the whole time. I do not mean to imply by this, however, that she was just a solid country lass.

She had tied the red obi[1] which was around her waist with a simplicity which suggested a young girl's indifference as to whether or not it enhanced her charms. Carrying an old-fashioned taper in her hand, she had led me to the bathhouse now this way now that, around bend after bend along what appeared to be passageways, and down flights of

---

[1] A wide sash often knotted intricately at the back.

stairs. In front of me all the time were that same red obi and that same taper, and it seemed as though we were going along the same passage and down the same staircase again and again. Already I had the feeling of being a painted figure moving about on a canvas.

When she had come to serve supper, she had apologised for putting me in one of the family rooms, but had said that since nobody had been there recently, the guest rooms had not been dusted. Now, having made my bed, she wished me good night, and went out of the room. Her voice was certainly human enough, but in spite of this, in the silence that followed, after I had heard her footsteps gradually receding along those winding corridors and down those flights of stairs, I suddenly had the uncanny impression that there was not a living soul in the whole place.

Only once before had I ever had such an experience. A long time ago I went from Tateyama right across the province of Boshu to the Pacific coast, and then following the coastline I walked from Kazusa to Chosi. One evening during the trip I stopped somewhere and asked if I could put up there for the night. I say somewhere because I can no longer remember the name of the inn, or whereabouts it was. In fact I am not even sure that it was an inn at all. It was a large high house in which two women lived all alone. In reply to my request to stay the night, the elder of the two said, 'Certainly,' and the younger one said, 'This way, please.' She led me to the centre of the house past one spacious room after another, each of which was in a state of dilapidation and disrepair. The ground floor in this part of the house was built on a split level, and I had to go up three steps to get to my room. Just as I was about to go from the passageway into the room, a clump of bamboo growing slantwise under the eaves was caught by the evening breeze, and brushed first against my shoulders, and then up the back of my neck. A shiver of fear ran through me.

The floor boards of the verandah were already badly decayed, and I remarked that next year the shoots would push their way through, and the room would be alive with bamboo. The young woman gave a broad grin, but went out without saying a word.

That night I was unable to sleep because of the bamboo rustling so near to where my bed was. I opened the shōji, and in the bright summer moonlight allowed my gaze to wander over the grass-grown expanse of the garden which, unhindered by fence or wall, ran right down to an overgrown bank. Beyond this the ocean roared, and its large breakers rolled in to threaten the security of the world of men. I could not close my eyes all night, but lay in my ineffective mosquito net tense and watchful until the dawn. This, I thought, might well be a scene from some story book.

Since that time I had been on many trips, but not until now on my first night in Nakoi, had I felt like that again.

I was lying dozing in bed when, opening my eyes, I happened to see high up on the wall a scroll in a red-lacquered frame. Even lying on my back as I was, I could read clearly the Chinese characters written on it. They said:

Bamboo sweeps across the stairs,
But no dust rises
For 'tis but a shadow.

It was signed 'Daitetsu'. I am by no means a connoisseur of art, but I have always loved the style of calligraphy of Takaizumi who was a priest of the Obaku sect.[1] Ogen, Sokuhi and Mokuan all have their good points too, but Takaizumi's writing is the boldest and most elegant of all. Looking at these characters on the scroll, I was certain that they had been written by Takaizumi, because of the light and shade in the strokes, and because of the movement of the

<hr>

[1] A part of the Zen sect of Buddhism.

brush. But the signature 'Daitetsu' showed that in fact I was mistaken. Perhaps, I thought, Daitetsu had also been a priest of the Obaku sect. If this were so, however, I could not account for the fact that the paper looked, so, extraordinarily new. Yes, there was no doubt about it, this scroll had been written very recently.

Looking sideways, my eyes lighted on a picture of a crane by Jakuchu hanging in an alcove. When I had first entered the room my professional instinct had told me immediately that this was a masterpiece. Most of Jakuchu's pictures are full of the most delicate colours, but this crane had been painted with one stroke of the brush, making no concession to popular taste. The way in which the egg-shaped body perched lightly on the one slender leg on which the crane was standing, showed that the artist had painted this to suit himself. His light-heartedness and disregard for convention were expressed right down to the tip of the bird's beak. Next to the alcove was a simple arrangement of shelves, and then an ordinary cupboard. I wondered what was in there.

I began to drift gently into sleep and into dreams.

There was the maid of Nagara with her long billowing sleeves, riding a white horse through a mountain-pass, when out leapt the two men Sasada and Sasabe, and each tried to drag her off. Suddenly the girl turned into Ophelia; first climbing out along the branch of a willow, and then being carried away by the stream, singing in a beautiful voice. Thinking to save her, I grabbed a long pole and ran after her along the shore of Mukōjima.[1] She did not seem in the least unhappy, but smiling and singing drifted with the current down to wherever it would take her. I put the pole on my shoulder, and yelled, 'Hey, come back! Come back!'

---

[1] An island near Tokyo.

43

At this point I awoke to find that I was damp with perspiration under the arms. What a strange conglomeration of the poetic and commonplace that dream had been, I thought. Long ago during the Sung dynasty in China a Buddhist priest named Ta Hui said that having attained a state of supreme enlightenment, there was nothing he could not do if once he set his mind to it. Nevertheless, he was a victim of mundane thoughts in his dreams, and for a long time this caused him a great deal of suffering. I can quite imagine how he felt. It must have seemed to a man who had devoted his whole life to the arts, that not to be able to dream beautiful dreams was a sign of still being shackled by the world. I felt that most of my last dream was material for neither a picture nor a poem. Turning over in bed to try to get to sleep again, I saw that the moon was now shining on the shōji, casting on them oblique shadows of two or three branches of the tree outside. What a beautifully fresh and crisp spring night it was.

I thought that it was perhaps just my fancy, but I had the feeling that somebody was singing softly. I strained my ears to try and determine whether a song had broken out of my dreams into reality, or whether this was a real voice which, because of my drowsiness, seemed to have been drawn into the obscurity of some distant land of dreams. Yes, somebody was definitely singing. The voice was undeniably thin and low, but nevertheless there it was, a gentle pulse rippling through the spring night which was all but asleep. The strange thing is, however, not that I heard the tune, but that when I listened for the words they came to me clearly, although there was no reason why they should have done, since they were not being sung anywhere near where I was sleeping. They were the words of the maid of Nagara's song, and seemed to be repeated over and over again.

From leaves of autumn flushed with love,
A pearl of dew shakes free

And falls to shatter on the earth beneath.
So too must I, to flee Love's stifling folds,
Drop from the world.

The voice had at first sounded near the verandah, but had now faded away into the distance. It is true that when something comes to an end suddenly it gives a feeling of suddenness, but you do not, however, feel the loss too keenly. When a voice ceases cleanly and decisively, it arouses a corresponding feeling in the listener. However, when faced with a phenomenon like this song, which can go on and on becoming fainter and fainter until eventually it disappears without your realising it, you find yourself breaking the minutes up into seconds and dividing the seconds into fractions, trying to pinpoint the exact time at which it will end; and all the time the pain caused by the anticipation of the loss grows more and more acute. It is like being with a sick man who appears ever on the verge of death but never dies, or watching a flame which gutters continually but never quite goes out. It throws your feelings into complete confusion, and drives out every thought save the one: Is this the end? Is this the end? There was something in this song which embodied all the regrets of mankind at the transience of spring in this ephemeral world.

Until now I had resisted the temptation to get up, and had lain quietly in bed, but as the voice went farther and farther away it seemed to call to me more and more strongly. I knew it was luring me on, but nevertheless I wanted to follow. The fainter it grew the more I longed to rush headlong after it, so that even if I could not be where it was, at least my ear could keep track of it, and it would not be lost to me completely. Just then, it seemed that the next instant, however pleadingly I might listen, there would be no response, and unable to bear it any longer, I slipped out of bed in spite of myself and slid back the shōji. As I did so the lower part of my body from the

45

knees down was bathed in moonlight, and the wavering shadow of a tree fell slantwise across me.

I did not of course notice such things as these immediately upon opening the shōji. I peered straight ahead of me in the direction from which my probing ear told me the voice was coming. There reclining against the trunk of what, judging by the blossoms, I took to be an aronia, was a dim shadow which appeared to shun *all* contact with the moonlight. I had my wits about me sufficiently to notice this, but before it could really register properly, the black shape moved sharply away to the right, crushing the shadows of blossom underfoot as it went. I had a fleeting glimpse of the tall smoothly gliding figure of a woman, before she was hidden from view by an angle of the overhanging roof.

I stood there in a daze with my hand still on the shōji, clad only in the yukata[1] that had been laid out for me. Presently, however, as I came to myself, it was born in upon me just how cold spring can be in the mountains. 'Well, that's that,' I thought, and climbing back in between the sheets, I fell to thinking. I pulled out my watch from under the pillow and looked at the time. Ten past one. I pushed it back under the pillow again and returned to my thoughts. What I had seen could not possibly have been an apparition. If not an apparition then, it must have been human; and if human it must have been a woman. Perhaps it was Shioda's daughter. If this were so, however, I did not consider it exactly the height of propriety that she, a woman divorced from her husband and now back living with her father, should, in the middle of the night, be out in the garden running as it did straight out on to the mountainside. It was no good, I just could not sleep. I lay there listening to the tick-tick-tick-tick of the watch under my pillow. I had never before been troubled by the ticking of a watch,

---

[1] A light-weight kimono, sometimes used to sleep in.

but that night it sounded as though it were saying, 'Think-think-think-think, think-think-think-think,' and repeating the same piece of advice over and over again: 'Don't-sleep-don't-sleep, don't-sleep-don't-sleep.' Confound it!

Even something frightening may appear poetic if you stand back and regard it simply as a shape, and the eerie may make an excellent picture if you think of it as something which is completely independent of yourself. Exactly the same is true with disappointed love. Providing that you can divorce yourself from the pain of a broken heart and, conjuring up before you the tenderness, the sympathy, the despair and yes, even the very excess of pain itself, can view them objectively, then you have aesthetic, artistic material. There are those who purposely imagine their hearts to be broken, and crave for the pleasure they get from this form of emotional self-flagellation. The average person dismisses them as foolish, or even a little mad, but there is absolutely no difference, inasmuch as they both have an artistic standpoint, between the man who draws an outline of misery for himself and then leads his life within it, and him whose delight it is, to paint a landscape which never existed, and then to live in a potted universe of his own creation. This being the case then, there are many artists who, outside their everyday lives, in the role of artist are more foolish, more insane than the ordinary man. We tramp around the countryside in search of suitable material, continually complaining from morning till night of the hardships we have to undergo. When, however, we are describing our journey to someone else, we show not even the slightest hint of discontent. Not only do we tell of the interesting and pleasant things that happened to us, which is only natural, but we even babble on proudly about those hardships long ago of which at the time we complained so bitterly. This is not done with any conscious intent of deceiving or cheating the listener. The inconsistency arises because while actually on the journey our feelings are just the same as those of anyone else. It is only afterwards when we tell our experiences to others that we revert to being artists. Putting it as a formula, I suppose you could say that an artist is a person who lives in the triangle which remains after the angle which we may call common sense has been removed from this four-cornered world.

Because of this lack of common sense, the artist is not afraid to approach those areas, both in the natural and in the man-made world, from which the average person shrinks back, and in consequence is able to find the most exquisite pearls of beauty. This portrayal of beauty where it is commonly believed that none exists, is generally called 'poetic embellishment'. It is nothing of the sort. There is, in fact, no need for embellishment, since in all things there lies beneath the surface an intrinsic beauty which is a reality, and which has always existed in all its brilliance merely waiting to be discovered. The reason why nobody appreciated the beauty there is in a steam engine before Turner depicted it on canvas, or realised that a ghost may be a thing of beauty until Ohkyo pointed it out to them, is threefold. First, most people walk around in a stupor, half blinded by the mundane nature of their thoughts; secondly, the fetters and bars of mediocrity make this world a difficult place to break out of; and finally, the man in the street is constantly being goaded by worries of whether or not such and such will get him a good reputation, or whether a certain course of action will be to his advantage.

The shadow I had just seen, considered simply as a shadow and nothing more, was charged with poetry. So much so, that nobody who saw or heard it could possibly fail to appreciate the fact.—A hot-spring in a secluded village—the shadow of blossoms on a spring night—a voice singing softly in the moonlight—a figure flitting through the shadows—every one of them a subject to delight any artist. Yet for all that I had engaged in an investigation which was quite out of keeping with the situation, and probed about pointlessly trying to find reasons for everything. I had been privileged to see the world of pure poetry, and had tried to apply to it the yardstick of logic. Moreover, all because of an unpleasant sensation, I had ridden roughshod over the rarest delicacy and elegance crushing them into the ground. My claim to be able to rise above human emotions then, was obviously nothing more than idle boasting. I should still have to discipline myself more before I could say with any confidence that I was a poet or an artist. I remember hearing once that long ago an Italian painter named Salvador Rosa was so set on studying the ways of robbers that he risked his life by joining a band of mountain brigands. It was a shameful thing if I, having wandered off suddenly from home with just a sketchbook tucked inside my kimono, did not have the same amount of resolution.

How, I wondered, could you regain a poetical frame of mind at times like this? I came to the conclusion that it could be done, if only you could take your feelings and place them in front of you, and then taking a pace back to give yourself the room to move that a bystander would have, examine them calmly and with complete honesty. The poet has an obligation to conduct a post-mortem on his own corpse and to make public his findings as to any disease he may encounter. There are many ways in which he may do this, but the best, and certainly the most convenient, is to try and compress every single incident which he comes across into the seventeen syllables of a Hokku. Since this is poetry in its handiest and most simple form, it may be readily composed while you are washing your face, or in the lavatory, or on a tram. When I say that it may be readily composed, I do not mean it in any derogatory sense. On the contrary, I think it is a very praiseworthy quality, for it makes it easy for one to become a poet; and to become a poet is one way to achieve supreme enlightenment. No, the simpler it is, the greater its virtue. Let us assume that you are angry: you write about what it is that has made you lose your temper, and immediately it seems that it is someone else's anger that you are considering. Nobody can be angry and write a Hokku at the same time. Likewise, if you are crying, express your tears in seventeen syllables and you feel happy. No sooner are your thoughts down on paper, than all connection between you and the pain which caused you to cry is severed, and your only feeling is one of happiness that you are a man capable of shedding tears.

This was what I had always claimed, and now I was going to try and put my theory into practice. Lying in bed I started to write a series of Hokku about the night's happenings. Since this was to be a serious venture, I lay my sketchbook open next to the pillow so that I could write down the lines as soon as they came to me. I knew that if I did not do this my mind would go off at a tangent, and they would be lost.

Aronia blossoms decked with dew:
Fool would he be who shook the bough.

These were the lines I wrote first. Although when I read them through I did not find them particularly engaging, neither did I find them too unpleasant. I next wrote:

The shadows of a spring night blend and blur,
But there amidst the blossoms I feel sure
A woman stands.

I felt that this captured the feeling of a spring night, but expressed nothing else. It did not trouble me, however, since all I really wanted to do was to help myself relax. My third attempt was:

> Fox or woman, woman or fox
> That figure in the misty moonlight standing?[1]

I thought that this was rather like comic verse, and even though I had written it myself, I found it amusing. Things were going very nicely I thought, and warming to my subject, I scribbled the following lines as fast as they came into my head.

> Not blossoms but the midnight stars of spring she plucks,
> And weaves them into garlands for her hair.

> She stands, damp hair just washed cascading down her
>   back,
> Streaking the clouds on this spring night with beauty.

> Spring! And from a shadow comes a voice
> Bestowing on the night the gift of song.

> The spirit of the aronias that must be
> Which on this moonlit night has ventured forth.

> The song now flows, now gently ebbs away,
> Wandering through the springtime 'neath the moon.

> There she stands so utterly alone,
> And beaten Spring draws slowly to its close.

As I read these lines through, I became sleepy and began to doze.

Perhaps spellbound is the best word to describe the condition I was in. Nobody can be conscious of himself when he is fast asleep, just as no one can ignore the world around him when he is wide awake. There lies, however, between these two states, a strip of no-man's land in which you cannot be said to be awake, since everything is too obscure, yet on the other hand you are not asleep for a small spark of life still remains. It is as though 'awake' and 'asleep' had been poured into the same jar and stirred with the brush of poetry, until thoroughly mixed.

---

[1] The fox in Japanese legends often assumes human guise.

Imagine the bright colours of Nature shaded off until they almost, but not quite, fade into a dream; or, this clear-cut world adrift in a sea of mist. Use the magic hand of sleep to smooth off all the sharp corners from reality, and then set it, thus tempered, gently pulsating. This is the state I mean. In such a condition your soul is just like smoke which, crawling along the ground, seems always on the point of rising into the air but never quite manages to do so. It tries to leave your body, but cannot bear the parting. Again and again it is on the verge of breaking out, but hesitates every time. Always at the last moment it fights to remain an entity, and twines itself about you lest its vast energy should be dissipated. Eventually, however, you feel its grip growing weaker and weaker.

It was while I was wandering in this no-man's-land of semi-consciousness that I heard the door of my room slide open. There in the doorway the phantom-like shape of a woman gradually materialised. I was neither surprised nor alarmed, but felt quite at ease as I lay there looking at her. I say 'looking at', but that is too strong a word, for actually she had slipped behind my closed eyelids. The apparition glided into the room, but I could hear no sound of footfalls on the matted floor. She was like some sprite moving on the surface of the water. Her skin was pale, and she had a wealth of jet-black hair which ran tapering to a point down the nape of her long graceful neck. Since my eyes were half closed, the overall effect was of holding up to the light one of those vignettes which are all the fashion nowadays.

The figure stopped in front of the cupboard. The door opened, and in the darkness I caught a glimpse of white as a pale arm emerged slowly from its sleeve. The door of the cupboard closed again, and the floor of my room, rising and falling in waves, bore the figure back to the doorway. As she passed through, the door slid itself shut behind her. My eyelids became heavier and heavier, and sleep gradually stole over me. I think that the condition I was in must have been very like that of a person who, having died, is in a period of suspension before being reborn into perhaps a cow or a horse.

How long I slept, wandering between man and horse, I do not know, but eventually I was awakened by the sound of a woman laughing. Opening my eyes, I saw that the curtain of night had long since been drawn aside, and the whole world was light again. The glorious spring sunshine had painted a dark lattice-work of bamboo on the shōji. As I looked out at the world through the circular window let into the shōji, it seemed that there was nowhere left for anything eerie to hide itself. My mysterious apparition had presumably returned to the land from which it had come, far far away across the Styx.

I got up, and went down to the bath-room just as I was. I lay back leisurely in the bath for about five minutes, just keeping my face above water, having neither the energy to wash myself, nor to get out. Why, I wondered, had I felt so peculiar last night. It was extraordinary, I thought, that just crossing the boundary from day into night should cause the world to fall into such utter confusion.

I felt very fit, but could not be bothered to dry myself. Still wet, therefore, I walked over to the bath-room door and opened it, thus letting myself in for another shock.

'Good morning. Did you sleep well last night?'

This was said at almost the exact instant that I opened the door. I had not expected to find anybody on the other side of the door, so this greeting, coming suddenly as it did, took me by surprise. Before I had a chance to reply, the person who had just spoken went round behind me.

'There you are, slip this on.' So saying she draped a beautifully soft kimono around me. Gradually I pulled myself together enough to say:

'Er . . . thank you . . . er . . .' I turned round to say this, and as I did so the woman drew back a little.

It has long been an established principle that the novelist must describe the looks of his hero or heroine in the most minute detail. If all the words and phrases which have been employed for this purpose by Western and Oriental writers from classical until modern times were collected together, they might well rival the great Buddhist Sutras in volume. Moreover, were I merely to pick out from this terrifyingly large number of epithets all those which adequately described the woman who was now standing there a little apart from me, they would make a list I know not how long. She held her body inclined at an angle, and was looking at me contemptuously as though enjoying my discomfort. Never in all my thirty years of life had I ever seen such an expression on anyone's face.

According to artists, the ancient Greek ideal of sculpture was to produce a figure which embodied what may be summed up as 'energy in repose'. That is to say a figure in which vital energy is on the point of being, but has not quite been motivated. The attraction of such a figure never palls, but becomes greater the more you look at it, for you always wonder what this energy would become were it unleashed: a whirlwind perhaps, or thunder and lightning. Thus it is that Greek art has continued to hold a wealth of meaning for generation after generation down through the centuries. Were the figure to move, all the great dignity of mankind which is dormant in the enormous potential force would be expressed. In the course of expressing this, however, the figure would be forced to change to some other position in which a different set of conditions prevailed. Admittedly every one of these new positions would have its own individual potentiality, but once having moved, the figure could never again return to its original state of harmony. Any new situation would be as ugly as that resulting were a beautiful river to subside suddenly, revealing a bed of mud. It is for this reason that I think that wherever you have motion, you must also have vulgarity. The reason for the failure of Hokusai's comic pictures, and Unkei's statues of the two Nio[1] lies in this one word 'motion'. Motion or repose? That is the burning question which governs the fate of us artists. One ought, more or less, to be able to put the qualities of beautiful women through the ages into one or other of these categories.

Looking at this woman's features, however, I felt at a loss, and was unable to decide. She stood there quietly, her mouth set in a thin line, and her eyes darting about restlessly, as though anxious not to miss even the smallest detail. In contrast to the fullness and composure of the lower part of her classically oval face, her forehead was narrow and formed a so-called widow's peak in the centre. Her eyebrows, moreover, almost met together, and twitched fretfully as though there were a drop of mint oil drying between them and causing a cold tingling sensation. Her nose was in perfect proportion, being neither too sharp and flippant, nor too round and dull. It would have made a beautiful picture. Considered separately, each one of her features had a distinct characteristic of its own, but all crowding in upon me in mad confusion as they were, it is no wonder that I felt bewildered.

Picture yourself standing on a piece of solid ground which until now you have always considered to be safe. Suddenly, it starts to buck and heave throwing you this way and that, and there is nothing you can do about it. Realising that such violent movement is unnatural to you, you do your uttermost to regain your former stance. All your efforts, however, are

---

[1] Two mythological strong kings, who were bodyguards to the goddess Kwannon.

thwarted by the impetus of the original shock-wave which first threw you off balance, and you continue to move against your will. You are just on the point of giving up hope, and of resigning yourself to the fact that you will be forced to keep moving indefinitely. If you can imagine what your expression would be like in such a situation, then you know just how that woman standing before me looked.

Thus it was that behind the look of contempt I could see a desire to cling to someone, and beneath her sneering attitude I caught a glimpse of prudence and good sense. She tried to appear as though if she gave free rein to her wit and high spirits she could handle a hundred men with ease, but in spite of herself she could not contain the gentle compassion which seeped through the hard exterior. There was absolutely no consistency in her expression. She was a person in whom understanding and bewilderment were living together under the same roof and quarrelling. This lack of consistency in her expression was evidence of the conflicting nature of her feelings, which in turn reflected the instability of the life she had lived. Hers was the face of one who is oppressed by misfortune, but is struggling to overcame it. She was undoubtedly a very unhappy woman.

'Thank you.' I repeated the words with a slight bow.

'Ha, ha, ha, ha, ha.—Your room has been dusted. Go and have a look. I'll come and see you later.'

So saying, she turned lightly on her heel and hurried away along the passage. Her hair was swept up in a high, butterfly-shaped style which revealed her slender white neck.

That black obi she is wearing is probably only *faced* with satin.

✦ 4 ✦

I wandered absently back to my room, and saw that, as she had said, it had been tidied and dusted. I still felt a little uneasy about what had happened the night before, and so I had a look in the cupboard just to put my mind at rest. In the lower part there was a small chest of drawers from the top of which trailed part of a printed muslin sash. This suggested that somebody might have come and taken some clothes or something in a hurry. The upper part of the sash disappeared from view into the folds of some delightfully feminine kimono. At the side of the chest was a small pile of books. The top one was *Orategama* by the Chinese Buddhist priest Haku-un, and under this was a copy of the classic *Tales of Ise*. Perhaps what I had seen the night before had not been an apparition after all, I thought.

I sat down aimlessly on a cushion in front of the low table which was made of ebony or some such expensive foreign wood. Then it was that my eye chanced to fall on my sketchbook. It looked very impressive lying there open, with a pencil still between the leaves. I wondered how those poems that I had feverishly scribbled down last night would look in the cold light of day.

Aronia blossoms decked with dew:
Fool would he be who shook the bough.

I was surprised to see that beneath this someone had written:

57

> Aronia blossoms decked with dew:
> Disturbed as dawn's light perches on the bough.

This had been written in pencil, and was therefore rather difficult to read. The writing looked too firm to be a woman's, and too graceful to be a man's. I looked at my next poem.

> The shadows of a spring night blend and blur,
> But there beneath the blossoms I feel sure
> A woman stands.

Underneath this had been written:

> The shadows of a spring night blend and blur
> And blossoms and woman are as one.

> Fox or woman, woman or fox
> That figure in the misty moonlight standing?

This had been amended to:

> Lord or lady, lady or lord
> That figure in the misty moonlight standing?

Had these been written in an attempt to copy my poems, to improve them, or as an expression of agreement with my taste? Were they foolish, or were they meant to make me feel foolish? I just did not know.

She had said that she would come and see me later, so she might arrive at any minute, or when my meal was brought. Anyway, I thought, when she did come, I would get more idea of why she had written the poems. Thinking of the meal made me wonder what time it was. Looking at my watch I saw that it was after eleven o'clock. I really had had a good sleep. Missing breakfast and just getting up in time for lunch was probably good for my stomach, I reflected.

I slid back the shōji on the right-hand side of my room, and looked out into the garden, trying to determine where the events of the night before, which still haunted me, had actually taken place. I had been right about the tree, it was indeed an aronia, but the garden was larger than I had thought. Peeping out from the thick carpet of green moss, which, they say, is so delightful to walk on barefooted, were five or six stepping stones. Off to the left, a red pine growing among some rocks leaned out over the garden from a steeply rising cliff face. Beyond the aronia was a small thicket, from the centre of which a clump of tall bamboo stems stretched their green lengths up and up, basking in the spring sunshine. My view to the left was interrupted by the ridge of the roof, but nevertheless it was obvious from the general layout of the place, that the ground dipped gently down to the bath-house.

The mountain sloped down to become a hill, and the hill sloped down to a level strip of land about a quarter of a mile in width. This in its turn shelved down into the sea and rose again sharply forty miles away to form the island of Maya-jima, which was about fifteen miles in circumference. Such then was the geography of Nakoi. The hot-spring hotel had been closely terraced against the foot of the hill, and its garden extended about half way up, making full use of the rugged scenery. This made it seem that house and hillside were but a single unit; the one complementing the other. There were two storeys at the front, but only one at the back, so sitting on the verandah and dangling my legs over the edge, I was easily able to touch the moss below. I could now see why I had had to go up and down all those flights of stairs, and why I had thought that the house was so strangely planned.

Next I walked over to the left hand side of the room, and opened the window. At some time or other water had collected in a natural hollow about six feet by six, and now its calm surface held the reflection of a wild cherry tree. Two or three small bushes of variegated bamboo growing around the corner of the rock added further colour to the scene. Some way off, I could see a hedge of what looked like box-thorn. Occasionally I heard the sound of voices coming from the other side, where there appeared to be a track running up the steep hillside from the beach. Beyond this track orange trees grew on the gentle southern slope which ran down to a large bamboo grove gleaming whitely in the sunlight. I had never realised before that bamboo leaves have this silvery sheen when seen from a distance. Across the valley, the hillside above the bamboo grove was covered with pine trees, and between the red trunks five or six stone steps were clearly visible. Probably, I thought, they led up to a temple.

Pulling back the shōji, I stepped out on to the verandah which, I found, ran all the way round an inner court. Opposite me on the first floor of the front part of the house, was a room from which I thought, if my sense of direction were right, the sea ought to be visible. It amused me to realise that although technically on the ground floor, judging by the rail of the verandah, the room in which I was living, and that room across there were at the same height. In fact from the point of view of anyone taking a bath, I was on the dizzy heights of the second floor, since the bath house was below ground level.

The house was very large, but except for the room opposite, one room on the same floor as mine in the right wing of the house, and possibly also the family's rooms and the kitchen, everywhere was shut up. This seemed to suggest that, apart from myself, there were scarcely any guests. Even though it was broad daylight, nearly all the shutters were still closed, and should anybody ever go so far as to open them, I doubted very much if they would close them again at night. I was not even sure whether or not they locked the front door. This was an ideal place for someone like myself who was trying to get away from the world.

It was almost twelve o'clock by my watch, but there was

still no sign of anything to eat. It gradually dawned on me just how hungry I was. Suddenly, however, a line from a Chinese poem came into my head. 'Totally alone upon the barren mountainside', and imagining myself to be in just such a situation I forgot all about food. Indeed it seemed that it might not be a bad thing to miss a meal. It was too much trouble to paint, and it seemed ludicrous to write a Hokku, when there I was immersed in that blissful state of self-forgetfulness which is itself poetry. I thought that perhaps I might read, but I could not bring myself to fetch the two or three books which were tied to my tripod. It seemed to me, lying there leisurely among the shadows of blossoms on the verandah, and feeling the warmth of the spring sunshine on my back, that I was sampling the greatest delights that this world has to offer. I knew that if I were to think, I would be dragged off along some side track. It was dangerous to move. Had it been possible I would have even stopped breathing. I just wanted to stay there quietly for about a fortnight, as though I were a plant which had pushed its way up through the matted floor.

At last I heard someone walking up the stairs and along the passageways. As they came nearer, I thought that I could make out the steps of two people. No sooner had they stopped outside my door than one person walked away again without a word. I waited, expecting to see once more the woman I had met that morning in the bathroom. When the door slid back, however, it was not she that was standing there, but the young girl who had shown me to my room the night before. I felt somehow as though I had been cheated.

'Sorry to have kept you waiting.' So saying she placed a small portable dinner table in front of me. She made no excuse, however, for not having brought me any breakfast. On the table was a wooden bowl, and a plate of broiled fish garnished with parsley. Removing the lid, I saw that

61

the bowl contained clear soup at the bottom of which I could see the pink and white of shrimps lying among some young ferns. I thought the colours so lovely that for a while I just sat there staring into the bowl.

'Don't you like it?' the girl asked.

'Oh yes, I like it. I'll eat it in a moment,' I replied; but to tell the truth I thought it a great pity to eat something which was so delightful to look at. I remember reading a story about Turner in an art book once. It seemed that one evening at a dinner he gazed for a long time at the salad on his plate, and then remarked to the person sitting next to him that he found its colour cool and refreshing, and that it was one which he often used. I just wished that I could have let Turner see the colour of those shrimps and ferns. There is not a single Western dish, with perhaps the possible exception of salad and radishes, which could be said to have an attractive colour. What the nutritional value is I am unable to say, but from the artistic point of view their food is extremely uncivilized. Japanese food on the other hand, whether it be soup, hors d'oeuvres or raw fish is always beautiful. It is so pleasant to see that it is worth going to a tea-house just to look at the dishes laid out before you, even if you come away without eating a single mouthful.

'There's a young lady living here, isn't there?' I asked replacing the bowl on the table.

'Yes, sir.'

'Who is she?'

'The young mistress, sir.'

'Is there another older mistress then?'

'There was, but she died last year.'

'And the master?'

'Oh yes sir, he's still alive. The mistress is his daughter.'

'The young lady, you mean?'

'Yes, sir.'

'Are there any other guests?'

'No, sir.'

'Just me then?'

'Yes, sir.'

'What does the young mistress do with herself every day?'

'Well, she sews . . .'

'And?'

'She plays the samisen.'[1]

This was both unexpected and interesting.

'What else does she do?' I asked.

'She goes up to the temple.'

Another unexpected answer. I found this samisen playing and going to the temple rather strange.

'Does she go there to pray?'

'No sir, she goes to see the priest.'

'Is he learning to play the samisen then?'

'No, sir.'

'Well then, why does she go there?'

'She goes to see Daitetsu, sir.'

Now I began to understand. This must be the same Daitetsu who wrote the poem which was hanging on the wall. I thought when I first saw it that it had been written by a Zen priest. That book of Haku-un's in the cupboard must have been borrowed from him too.

'Does somebody normally use this room?'

'Yes sir, the mistress.'

'Then she must have been in here until I arrived last night?'

'Yes.'

'Oh, I'm sorry to have turned her out of her own room. By the way, why does she go to see Daitetsu?'

'I'm afraid I don't know.'

---

[1] A three-stringed Japanese musical instrument of the guitar family.

'What else?'

'I beg your pardon?'

'I mean, what other things does she do?'

'Many other things.'

'Such as?'

'I don't know.'

This brought the conversation to an abrupt end. At length I finished my meal, and the girl took the table away. As she slid open the door, I caught sight of the woman with the 'butterfly' hairstyle across the top of the shrubbery in the inner court. She was standing on the first-floor verandah with her elbows resting on the rail, and her face cupped in her hands. This pose, added to the fact that she was gazing intently at something below, made her look for all the world like a statue of Kwannon the omniscient goddess of mercy. Her present air of serenity was in complete contrast to her appearance that morning. Since she was looking downwards, it was impossible from where I was sitting to see the expression in her eyes. I wondered whether, if I could have seen them, she would have presented a different picture. Someone long ago once said apparently, that nothing speaks for a man better than his pupils. This is quite true, for the eye is the most expressive and vital organ in the human body, and will mirror your feelings however much you may try to conceal them. From beneath the rail on which the 'butterfly' was leisurely leaning, two real butterflies came dancing erratically upward, now drawing together, now fluttering apart again. This then was the scene that confronted me as the door slid back. The noise of the door, however, disturbed her, and looking up sharply from the butterflies, she turned her attention towards me. Her unwavering gaze shot through the air like a poisoned arrow, and struck me between the eyes. Before I could recover from my surprise, the young girl slid the screen across again. Immediately the complete lassitude of spring returned.

Once again I sprawled out full length on the floor, and very soon the following lines came drifting into my mind.

Sadder than the moon's lost light,
Lost ere the kindling of dawn,
To travellers journeying on,
The shutting of thy fair face from my sight.

Suppose for a moment that I had been in love with 'the butterfly', and been dying to meet her. Then I too would have written just such a poem to express the mingled feelings of joy and regret which, before I had time to be surprised, such a brief glimpse of her as I had just had would undoubtedly have aroused in me. I might also have added:

Might I look on thee in death,
With bliss I would yield my breath.[1]

Fortunately I had already left the triteness of falling in love far behind me, and could not have felt such pangs even if I had wanted to. Nevertheless, I thought that those few lines captured the poetry of the situation admirably. It was both amusing and pleasant to think of the poem as applying to 'the butterfly' and myself, and to pretend that it described our relationship, even though I knew that such a state of affairs was impossible. We were, it is true, joined together by a thin thread, because fate had decreed that I should see her in circumstances similar to those in which the poem had been written, thus making it partly real. Fate or no fate, however, so slender a tie could not prove painful. Moreover, this was no ordinary thread. It was as delicate as the rainbow spanning the sky, and as flimsy as mist trailing across the moors, or gossamer sparkling with dew; and

---

[1] Written by Soseki in English.

as such it was exceedingly beautiful to look at, but could be broken at will. Ah, but supposing that while I were looking at it, it should become as thick and strong as a hawser, what then? No, there is no fear of that happening. I am an artist, and she is not like the normal run of women.

Suddenly the door opened, and turning over on to my side I saw her standing there: 'the butterfly', the other end of the thread. She was carrying a tray on which was a green celadon porcelain bowl.

'Lying down again? It must have been very annoying for you to have been disturbed so many times last night. I'm afraid I was a terrible nuisance,' she said with a mischievous laugh. There was nothing at all timid or bashful about her, and of course no trace of embarrassment either. I felt that she was definitely ahead in the game.

'Thank you for what you did this morning.' When I came to think about it, I realised that this was the third time I had referred to her helping me on with the kimono that morning. Not only that, but each time all I had been able to get out was 'Thank you'.

While I was still trying to get up into a sitting position, she came over quickly and squatted down next to me.

'Oh, don't bother to sit up. We can talk perfectly well while you are lying down,' she said in an apparently friendly voice. I thought that this was perfectly true, so I just rolled over on to my stomach, and leaning on my elbows, rested my chin on my hands.

'I thought you might be bored, so I've come to make you some tea.'

'Thank you.'—There it was again.

Looking into the cake bowl which she had brought I saw that it contained some green 'yokan' made from bean jelly. I think that of all cakes, yokan are my favourite. It is not that I especially enjoy eating them, but I consider that their smooth fine texture, and the way in which they become semi-transparent when the light falls on them, makes them indisputably an *objet d'art*. These yokan were particularly pleasant to look at, for their green-tinged lustre made them look as though they were precious stones, or as though they had been fashioned from alabaster. They so matched the bowl in colour and in glaze, that it seemed as though the very porcelain itself had just given birth to them. As I looked at them, I had an overwhelming desire to stretch out my hand, and gently run my fingers over the glistening surfaces. There is not a single Western cake which can give one so much pleasure. Cream, I admit, has a soft colour, but for all that there is something rather heavy about it. Jelly looks like a jewel, but its trembling and shaking deprive it of the solidity of a yokan; while that intricately shaped heap of sugar and milk which they call blancmange is an absurdity which is beyond the power of words to describe.

'Hm—beautiful,' I said.

'Gembei brought them back with him just now. I hope you like them.'

Apparently then Gembei must have stayed overnight down in the town. I made no reply, but just continued to look at the yokan. I was not interested in where, or by whom they had been bought. It was enough for me merely to know that they were beautiful.

'I like the shape of this bowl very much. It has a lovely colour too. It's almost as beautiful as the yokan.'

The woman gave a short low laugh, and a vague flicker of contempt played about her mouth. I wondered if she had thought I was trying to be funny. Taken as a joke it certainly deserved scorn, for as such it was just the sort of remark that fools make when they are attempting to be clever.

'Is it Chinese?' I asked.

'Pardon?' She was not the least concerned with the bowl.

'Somehow it looks Chinese to me,' I went on, holding it up and examining the underside.

'Are you interested in that sort of thing? Would you like to see some more?'

'Yes, I would please.'

'Father is very fond of curios, and has all sorts of things. I'll tell him about you, and ask him to invite you to have a cup of tea sometime.'

When I heard the word 'tea', my enthusiasm waned a little. There is nobody as ostentatious, or as persuaded of his own refinement of taste as the man who performs the tea-ceremony.[1] He deliberately reduces the wide world of poetry to the most cramped and limiting proportions. He is self-opinionated, over-deliberate in his actions, and a fussy old woman about trifling niceties. Moreover he approaches the ceremony with unnecessary awe and respect, and goes into ecstasies as he drinks the frothy tea. If such a jumble of petty rules and regulations can be said to constitute elegance and good taste, then the boys in the regimental barracks at Azabu must be fairly wallowing in it. Oh yes, if this is true, then every mother's son of the 'right turn' and 'eyes front' brigade would make an exceptionally fine teaman. Those who take part in the tea-ceremony are really only tradesmen, merchants and the like who have not the first idea of what the words 'artistic taste' mean. They have swallowed whole the teachings of the great tea-ceremony master Rikyu, and without any sense of elegance, or indeed of purpose, merely go mechanicaly through the motions. By so doing, they convince themselves that they are men of refinement, but this is nonsense. All they are really doing is making fools of those who truly do have the ability to appreciate elegance.

[1] This is a ceremony in which tea is made and drunk according to a very intricate set of rules. It is said to foster self-discipline, and to give one a sense of refined beauty.

'When you say 'tea', do you mean the tea-ceremony?' I asked.

'Oh no, this is tea without any ceremony. You need not even drink it if you do not want to.'

'Well in that case, I'd be delighted.'

'Father loves to show off his nick-nacks, so . . .'

'You mean I ought to say how nice I think they are?'

'Well, he's growing old, and it pleases him to receive compliments.'

'All right, I'll praise them a little then.'

'You might even force yourself to praise them a lot.'

'Ha, ha, ha.—By the way, from your language I would say you were not a country girl.'

'Meaning that from my character you would say I was?'

'As far as character is concerned it's better to be a country girl.'

'Then I have something to be proud of.'

'You've lived in Tokyo though, haven't you?'

'Oh yes, in Kyoto too. I'm rather a vagabond. I've been all over the place.'

'Which do you like best, here or Tokyo?'

'There's no difference.'

'But surely life must be more comfortable in a quiet place like this?'

'Whether you are comfortable or not depends entirely upon your frame of mind. Life is whatever you think it is. What is the use of running away to the land of mosquitoes, because you are uncomfortable in the land of fleas?'

'But why not go to a land where there are neither mosquitoes nor fleas?'

'Is there such a country?' she said edging closer. 'If there is, show it to me. Go on, show it to me.'

'All right, I will if you like.' So saying, I took out my sketchbook, and drew a woman on horseback, looking at a mountainside covered with wild cherry trees. I finished it in a moment, so it could hardly be called a picture, just a rough impression.

'There you are, get into this picture. There are no mosquitoes or fleas here,' I said, and pushed the book right under her nose. I was sure that the situation would cause her neither surprise, embarrassment nor discomfort. I watched her for a moment. At length she passed it off by saying:

'What a cramped and uncomfortable world. It is all width and no depth. Do you like a place like this where the only way to move is sideways? You must be a regular crab.' This made me burst out laughing.

A nightingale came near the eaves and began to sing. Then breaking off in mid-song, he flew away and perched on the branch off a tree some distance away. We both stopped talking, and sat there for a while waiting to hear if the bird would sing again. It seemed, however, that he had lost his voice for good.

'I suppose you met Gembei up in the mountains yesterday?'
'Yes.'
'Did you go and see the maid of Nagara's tomb, the five-storied pagoda?'
'Yes.'
Suddenly, with no further preamble, the woman began to recite the words of the maid of Nagara's song in a flat even voice. I had no idea why.

From leaves of autumn flushed with love,
A pearl of dew shakes free
And falls to shatter on the earth beneath.
So too must I, to flee Love's stifling folds
Drop from the world.

'Ah,' I said, 'I heard that song up at the tea-house.'
'Did the old woman teach it to you? She used to be a

maid here. That was before I . . . .' Here she looked search-ingly at my face, so I pretended to know nothing.

'It was when I was still young,' she went on. 'Even when she was no longer employed here, she used to come and see me, and every time I would tell her that story. But she just could not learn the words of the song. Gradually, however, by hearing it over and over again, she managed to commit it all to memory.'

'Ah, that explains it. I wondered how she had come to learn something so difficult. But that's a sad song isn't it?'

'Yes, I suppose it is, but I would never have sung a song like that. In the first place the maid of Nagara gained nothing by throwing herself in the Fuchi river, did she?'

'No that's true. Well, what would you have done in her position?'

'What would I have done? I should have thought that was quite simple. I would merely have taken both Sasado and Sasabe as lovers.'

'What, both of them?'

'Yes.'

'That's very clever.'

'Not at all. It's the obvious thing to do.'

'I see. Well, that means that you would end up in neither the country of mosquitoes nor the country of fleas.'

'Well, it isn't necessary to adopt the mentality of a crab in order to carry on living.'

'Hoh—hokekyo—.' Our forgotten nightingale began to get his voice back, and in no time at all was sending forth the most unexpected high trills. Once he had got properly started again, the notes seemed to come more easily. Hanging upside down, and puffing out his throat, he vibrated it to the very depths as the notes burst from him. 'Hoh, hokekyo—, hoh, hokekyo—', on and on he ran.

'That is real poetry,' said the woman.

✦ 5 ✦

'Excuse me sir, but am I right in thinkin' you're from Tokyo?'

'Do I look as though I were?' I asked.

'Look? Why, I didn't have to look sir. I could tell you was from Tokyo as soon as I heard you speak.'

'Can you tell which part?'

'Well now, let me see. Tokyo is such a stupidly big place . . . . I should say it was one of the posher areas—like Kojimachi for instance, or Koishikawa maybe? Or else perhaps Ushigome or Yotsuya.'

'Hm yes, somewhere around there. You know Tokyo well, don't you?'

'Oh, yes sir. You wouldn't think it to see me here now, but I was born an' bred in Tokyo.'

'Ah, that explains it. I thought you looked a bit of a live wire.'

At this he let out a loud guffaw, and then suddenly became serious.

'But it's pitiful when a man comes down to this,' he said.

'Whatever made you drift into the country like this?'

' "Drift" is the right word sir. There's no gettin' away from that. That's just exactly what I have done. Well, it was like this: I was out of work, and just couldn't get a job for love nor money, so . . . .'

'Have you always had a barber's shop?'

'Oh, I don't own this place. I'm only an assistant here. What's that you say? Whereabouts in Tokyo was I. Well, there's this place called Matsunagachō over Kanda way—and a pokey filthy hole it is too, I can tell you. It's not the sort of place a gentleman like yourself would ever have heard of. But there's a bridge called Ryukanbashi near there . . . . What's that? Oh, you've never heard of that either. Hm, Ryukanbashi's quite well known . . . .'

'Hey, would you mind putting a little more soap on my face please, it's hurting rather.'

'Hurtin' sir? I'm very pertic'ler about shavin'. I never feel satisfied until I've gone over the face again like this against the grain of the beard, so's I can prise each individual hair out of its hole.—No, the trouble with your modern barber is that 'e don't shave you, 'e just tickles you with the razor. Just bear it a bit longer, sir.'

'Bear it? That's exactly what I have been doing for a long time. Rub some soap on, or at least some warm water—please.'

'You mean you can't stand it no longer? It didn't ought to hurt as much as that. The trouble is you've let your beard grow too long.'

He had been pinching a lump of my cheek like grim death, but now with a show of reluctance he released it, and taking down a meagre piece of red soap from a shelf, ran it once over the whole of my face, having first given it a quick flick in some water. To have a piece of soap applied to my face directly, was not the sort of treatment I was used to in a barber's shop, and I must confess I did not like it much. Moreover when I looked at the water in which the soap had been dipped, I shuddered to think how long it had been standing there.

I was now required to exercise that privilege to which every customer in a barber's is entitled: namely that of inspecting himself in the mirror. This, however, is a right which since

I had come into the shop I had thought I might well dispense with. A mirror is failing in its obligations unless it has an even surface, and presents a truthful image of one's face. The man who hangs a mirror which is not possessed of these qualities on the wall, and then urges you to look at yourself in it, is just as guilty of wilfully damaging your appearance as the man who says he is an expert photographer and then produces a bad picture of you. It may well be that snubbing vanity is one means of improving the character, but nevertheless, to show someone his face at less than its true value, and then to have the audacity to say, 'this is you', is unnecessarily insulting. The unavoidable mirror into which I was expected to gaze with tolerance, had most decidedly been insulting me from the very outset. When I moved my head to the right my face became all nose, and when I moved it to the left my mouth became a slit which extended right up to my ears. If I lay back, I looked like the front view of a completely flattened toad; and if I leaned slightly forward, my body became foreshortened, and my head swelled up like a balloon. All the time I was in front of the mirror, I was continually changing from one monster into another. Admittedly the face which the mirror had to reflect was not very handsome, but I came to the conclusion that the monstrosity before me was produced by a combination of the mirror's faulty construction, and the fact that in places the silvering had peeled off at the back. I was not concerned by the visual abuse which was being hurled at me, but as I am sure anyone else would have done, I found it unpleasant to have to sit before my warped tormentor for any length of time.

This was no ordinary barber. When I first peeped into the shop, I saw him sitting there cross-legged, apparently very bored. He was pulling hard on a long pipe and puffing the smoke out at a toy flag of the Anglo-Japanese alliance. There is, I admit nothing strange in this, but it was after I had entered the shop and committed my head to his care that I first became disconcerted. The unpardonable fashion in which he handled my head while he was shaving me caused me to have grave doubts as to whether all rights of its ownership had passed to him, or whether I still retained some small say in the matter. I felt sure that even were it nailed on to my shoulders, it would not remain there long.

The way in which he set about wielding the razor made it quite clear that he knew nothing at all of the laws of civilization. The razor scraped across my cheek, and as it worked up towards my ear, the artery in my temple started throbbing so wildly that I thought it would burst. Next he moved down to my chin, where his flashing sword produced the weirdest crunching noises, like someone walking over icy ground. The terrible thing was that he considered himself the finest barber in the country.

To make a bad situation worse, the man was drunk. Everytime he said 'Si—ir', my nostrils were assailed by an unusually potent gas. At this rate, I thought, the razor is liable to take matters into its own hands. Since even the barber himself had no idea as to where he was going or what he was doing, it was completely impossible that I, who had merely lent him my face, should have the slightest notion. Since my face had been entrusted to him as the result of a mutual understanding, I did not intend to complain about any discomfort or even a slight nick with the razor, but what worried me was that he would suddenly have a brainstorm and I would end up with my throat cut.

'Only them as has no experience uses soap for shavin', sir. But p'raps in your case it can't be helped, 'cos you've really got a tough beard.' So saying he put the piece of soap, thin as it was, back up on the shelf. The soap, however, chose to disobey his orders, and immediately tumbled down on to the floor.

'I don't recall havin' seen you around here sir. Have you been here long?'

'Only about two or three days.'

'Ah. Whereabouts are you stoppin'?'

'At Shioda's.'

'Oh, you're a guest there, are you? I thought p'raps you might be. To tell you the truth, it was through old Mr Shioda that I got this job down here. Yes, I knew him back in Tokyo. Used to live in the same area. He's a good sort, and he's got his head screwed on the right way. He lost his wife last year, and now all he does is mess about with them there curios of his. They say he's got some marvellous stuff which'd fetch a tidy penny if it was sold.'

'He's got a beautiful daughter, hasn't he?'

'You want to watch out there.'

'Why, is there . . . . ?'

'Why? Well it was long before you came here sir, but she's divorced, that's why.'

'Really?'

'Is that all you've got to say, 'really'? I'm tellin' you she 'ad no business to leave 'er 'usband. It was just that the bank went broke, and because she couldn't play the lady any more, she up and left him. She's got no sense of gratitude. She's all right while the old man's alive, but nobody's goin' to look after her once he's gone.'

'No, I suppose not.'

'Stands to reason. I mean she don't get on with her elder brother, who lives in the family house, either.'

'Is there a family house?'

'Yes, it's up there on the hill. You ought to go up an' pay 'em a visit sometime. There's a lovely view from up there.'

'I say, go over with the soap again, will you? It's hurting again.'

'Shavin' do seem to hurt you, don't it sir? It's because

your beard's too tough. With whiskers like that you ought to shave every three days without fail. If it hurts when I shave you, it'd hurt you anywhere.'

'Well, I will in the future. I'll come and let you shave me every day.'

'Do you fancy stayin' here as long as that then sir? It's dangerous. Don't do it. No good can come of it, and who knows what trouble you'll land yourself in, if you get dragged into such a business.'

'Why?'

'Well, Shioda's daughter's pretty enough to look at, but she's not all there.'

'Why do you say that?'

'Why? Well sir, everybody in the village says she's mad.'

'There must be some mistake.'

'But we have proof. No, don't do it. It's too risky.'

'Don't worry about me. But tell me, what proof do you have?'

'Well, it's a funny story. Take it easy, an' have a cigarette, and I'll tell you about it.—Would you like your hair washed?'

'No, that's all right thanks.'

'Well, I'll just give you a massage to get rid of the dandruff.'

Hereupon, the barber placed all ten fingers on my head, regardless of the fact that the nails were thick with dirt, and proceeded to agitate them violently backwards and forwards. I could feel his nails gouging each individual root. It was just as though a colossal rake were being pushed and pulled across my scalp at whirlwind speed. I do not know how many thousands of hairs there are on my head, but I was convinced that he was tearing up each one by the root, and raising angry weals all over the resulting exposed surface. The vibration was sufficient to pass right through my skull into the brain itself. By the time he had finished, I was suffering from concussion.

'How's that? That's better, isn't it?'

'You really do go at things tooth and nail, don't you?'

'Eh? A nice massage like that makes everybody feel better.'

'I feel as though my head had been pierced in several places.'

'As bad as that? It's this weather wot does it. You always feel tired in spring.—Have a fag sir. You must get fed up with yourself, bein' the only one at Shioda's. You must come and have a bit of a chat sometimes. Some'ow, if you're from Tokyo it's hard to talk to someone who isn't. Er, does the young lady come and entertain you then sir? The trouble with her is, she aint got the faintest idea of right an' wrong.'

'You started to say something about her just now, before you began poking holes in my head.'

'So I did. I don't know. I'm so scatter-brained, I'm always jumpin' from one topic to the other, without ever finishing a story properly. Well, as I was sayin', the priest fell head over heels in love with her . . . .'

'What priest?'

'Why, the young novice up at the Kankaiji temple.'

'You haven't mentioned anything about a priest yet, novice or otherwise.'

'Haven't I? I'm so terrible hasty. Well this priest was good-lookin' in a rugged sort of way. 'E was the type that women go for. Anyway, he fell head over heels in love with old Shioda's daughter, and at last wrote a letter to her.—Hang on a minute. Did he write, or did he go and see her? No, that's right, he definitely wrote her a letter. Now where was I?—Er . . . What was I goin' to say?—I'm a bit mixed up. Oh, yes. That's right, that's what happened. It came as a shock see, so . . . .'

'Who was shocked?'

'The woman, of course.'

78

'When she received the letter?'

'If she was the sort of woman to be shocked by a letter, it would at least show some modesty. But she don't shock that easy.'

'Then who was shocked?'

'Why he was when he went to tell her he loved her.'

'But I thought you said he didn't tell her.'

'Give me strength. You got it all wrong. It was gettin' the letter that was a shock.'

'Then it must have been the woman who was shocked after all.'

'No, no, no, the man!'

'Well, if it was the man, it must have been the priest.'

'That's right it was the priest.'

'Why was he shocked?'

'Why was he shocked? Well he was in the main hall of the temple, conductin' a service with the abbot, when she suddenly comes rushin' in . . . . Cor, ha, ha, ha. There's no gettin' away from it, she must be cracked and no mistake.'

'What happened then?'

'Well, she suddenly flings her arms round Taian's neck, and says, "If you really love me so much, let's make love here before Buddha."'

'Did she now?'

'Taian didn't know where to put his face. He was so ashamed at havin' written to a mad woman, that he crept away secretly that night, and died.'

'Died?'

'Well, I presume he died. He could hardly 'ave gone on livin', after havin' been shamed like that.'

'I don't know about that.'

'Maybe you're right. I suppose 'is dyin' wouldn't have looked too good: her bein' mad an' all. P'raps he's still alive.'

'That's a very interesting story.'

'Interestin' 's not the word for it. It set the whole village laughing fit to bust. But it shows you just how mad that woman is: she never took a blind bit of notice. A steady man like yerself ought to be alright sir, but her bein' what she is, it wouldn't be advisable to go flirtin' with her.'

'Oh, I'll be very careful. Ha, ha, ha, ha, ha.'

A spring breeze wafted up from the warm beach, bringing with it a hint of the sea, and making the short curtain across the entrance of the barber's shop stir sleepily. In the mirror I caught a fleeting glimpse of a swallow as, body aslant, he dived across the space beneath the curtain. An old man of about sixty or so was sitting under the eaves of the house opposite, silently shelling molluscs. Again and again there came the dull metallic clack of his knife striking the shell, and again and again the reddish meat fell into the obscurity of his basket, and a shell, glinting in the sunlight, was sent sailing two or three feet across the heat-hazy ground. I could not tell whether the huge heap which had been piled up there was of oyster, clam or razorshells. From time to time the mound would collapse, and some of the shells would sink down to the bottom of a sandy stream. It seemed to me as though they were falling off the edge of this unstable world, to be buried in some dark shadowy region beneath. No sooner had the old shells been buried, however, than new ones would take their place, and the mound would grow again beneath the willow tree. The old man had no time to think of anything but shellfish, and he just went on steadily casting shells on to the shimmering ground. It seemed as though his basket were bottomless, and his spring day an unending source of tranquillity.

The sandy stream ran under a small bridge scarcely twelve feet across, carrying the water of spring down towards the sea. There, where the spring river flowed out to meet the spring tide, fathom upon fathom of fishing nets had been hung up in uneven banks to dry in the sun. It was these, I suspected, which gave the warm smell of raw fish to the gentle breeze as it passed through their meshes on its way up to the village. Between the nets the surface of the sea showed grey, undulating sluggishly like molten lead.

This scenery and the barber had nothing at all in common, and had he been a more forceful personality, strong enough to impress me as powerfully as my natural surroundings, then I would surely have been struck by the incongruity of their co-existence. Fortunately, however, he was not a very striking character, and for all his brash city ways, and his caustic wit, he was certainly no match for the perfect harmony and serenity of Nature. He had persistently tried to shatter this aura with his interminable chatter, but so formidable was his opponent that he had been reduced to the level of a barely perceptible speck of dust hovering in a ray of spring sunshine. One is not aware of any conflict between things or people, however incompatible their strength and bulk or their physical and spiritual characteristics may be, unless they are both possessed of an equal power. Indeed, if the disparagement in power between the two is exceptionally great, then all conflict may gradually be erased and the energy which generated it be absorbed by a greater force. It is for this reason that the disciple sits at the feet of the master, that the man of low intelligence reveres the disciple, and oxen and horses become the obedient servants of the man of low intelligence. My barber was at the moment playing out some ridiculous farce, with the whole limitless scenery of springtime as his backdrop. He, who was doing his uttermost to destroy the tranquillity of spring, had only succeeded in adding to it. I felt that I had fallen into the company of a meddling fool. This braggart with all his cheap talk was no more than a component colour in the landscape, blending perfectly with his surroundings on that peaceful spring day.

Since, looked at in this light, the barber would have made a fine subject for a painting or a poem, I remained parked where I was, chatting with him about this and that, long after my shave was finished. While we were talking, a young priest popped his small head under the entrance curtain and said, 'Hullo. Shave, please.' He was wearing a white cotton kimono tied with a padded obi. Over the top of this was a loose robe of coarse material, which looked like a mosquito net. He seemed a very happy-go-lucky fellow.

'Ah, Ryonen. How are you? I bet you got a good tickin' off from the abbot for wastin' your time the other day.'

'Oh no I didn't. He said I'd done very well.'

'Oh, so he praised you for stoppin' to go fishin' while you was out on an errand, did he?'

'Yes. He said, "Ryonen, you were quite right to play on the way. It shows a maturity beyond your years."'

'And as I might have expected, his praise has given you a swelled head. Look at it; all lumps and bumps. It's a shockin' job to shave a freak of a head like this. I'll let you off this time; but don't come in again until you've kneaded it back into shape.'

'If it were in good shape, I'd go to a better barber.'

'Ha, ha, ha. Your head may be a queer shape, but it doesn't affect your tongue.'

'Yes, and your hand may not be very steady when you're working, but it doesn't stop you lifting a glass, does it?'

'Why, you young whippersnapper. Whose hand isn't . . .'

'I didn't say it, the abbot did. And don't get so angry; remember your age.'

'Huh! That's not funny.—Is it, sir?'

'Hm? What?' I said.

'Confounded priests. Bloody well livin' up there high above the stone steps, with nothin' to do, and all day to do it in. I suppose that's why they all have such a ready tongue. Even this baby priest here doesn't mind what he says. Hey! Lean yer head back a bit—"Back," I said.—If you don't do as I tell you, you'll get cut. Understand? The blood will flow!'

'It hurts. You don't have to be so rough.'

'If you can't even stand this, how do you expect to become a priest?'

'I am a priest already.'

'Gercha, you're still only half-baked. By the way, how did Taian die?'

'He isn't dead.'

'Not dead? What do you mean? He must be.'

'After that business, he pulled himself together and went to the Daibanji temple in Rikuzen. He's devoted himself to his studies. Everyone says he's become very wise. It was a good thing that that happened to him.'

'What was good about it? I can't see that it's good, even for a priest, to take off in the middle of the night. You want to be careful. Women always bring you nothin' but trouble.—Talkin' about women, does "Nut-case" still come up to see the abbot?'

'I've never heard of a woman called "Nut-case".'

'You know who I'm talkin' about idiot. Does she, or doesn't she?'

'No "nut-case" as you call it comes; but Mr Shioda's daughter does.'

'She'll never get any better, however much the abbot prays for her. She's under a curse from her former 'usband.'

'Mr Shioda's daughter is a fine woman. The abbot speaks very highly of her.'

'I dunno. Everythin' up there above them stone steps is upside down. But I don't care what the abbot says; once mad, always mad.—Well, there you are: all shaved. Run along an' get another tickin' off.'

'No, I think I'll take my time so I'll be praised again.'

'Please yerself, you prattlin' imp.'

'Huh! You withered up piece of human refuse.'

'What did you say!'

But the newly shaven head, covered now only with dark blue shadow, had already darted beneath the curtain, and was being fanned by the spring breeze.

✦ 6 ✦

I had slid open all the imprisoning screens, and was sitting at
my desk in the fading twilight. The hotel was comparatively
large, and my room was separated from the region of human
activity where the few other occupants lived by innumerable
twisting corridors, with the result that no sound came to
disturb my thoughts. Today, things were particularly quiet.
I wondered perhaps whether the landlord, his daughter, the
young maid and the man servant had all slipped away some-
where without my knowing. If they had, I thought, it would
be no ordinary place to which they had gone, but a land of
haze or of clouds. Or possibly they had drifted far across a
languid sea, never touching the tiller, and not caring whether
or not they were moving, until they had reached that place
where sky and ocean meet, and where it becomes difficult to
distinguish the white sail from the clouds and the water, and
eventually even the sail is puzzled to know where to draw the
line between itself and its surroundings. It also occurred to
me that they might simply have vaporized and become part
of the spirit of spring. If this were so, then their hitherto
substantial forms would now be no more than haunting cur-
rents, swirling somewhere between heaven and earth, so
completely invisible that even with a microscope no trace of
them would be found. My next idea was that they had all
turned into larks and, having sung to their hearts' content,

translating the golden colour of spring rape-blossoms into music, had now flown off into the deep-purple folds of dusk. Or could they have lengthened the already long spring day by becoming gad-flies, to whom a day is a lifetime? Perhaps engrossed in their unsuccessful attempts at sipping the sweet dew from the stamens, they had been trapped beneath a falling camellia blossom, and were even now lying amidst the fragrance contentedly sleeping their lives away. Anyway, be that as it may, everything was completely quiet and still.

The spring breeze, which was passing drowsily through the empty house, came neither to gratify those who welcomed it, nor to spite those who wished to keep it out. It came and went quite naturally: an expression of the impartiality of the universe. I sat with my chin resting in my hands, thinking that if only my heart were as free and open as my room, the breeze would, unbidden, have found its way there too.

You are conscious of the ground you are standing on, and so fear that it may give way beneath you. You are aware that the heavens are above you, and so you quake with the fear of being struck by lightning. Life is an inescapable rat-race in which you are constantly being spurred on by materialistic values to wrangle and squabble with your neighbour. For us who live in this world with its East and West, and who have to walk the tight-rope of advantage and disadvantage, love which is free of self-interest is an enemy. And yet, visible wealth is as worthless as dust, and fame which has been avidly grasped is, it seems to me, like stolen honey which looked sweet while in the making, but in which the cunning bee has left his sting. The so-called pleasures in life derive from material attachments, and thus inevitably contain the seeds of pain. The poet and the artist, however, come to know absolute purity by concerning themselves only with those things which constitute the innermost essence of this world of relativity. They dine on the summer haze, and drink the evening dew. They discuss purple, and weigh the merits of crimson, and when death comes they have no regrets. For them, pleasure does not lie in becoming attached to things, but in becoming a part *of* them by a process of assimilation. And when at last they succeed in this, they find there is no room to spare for their ego. Thus, having risen out of the quagmire of material-ism, they are free to devote themselves to the real essentials of life, and thereby obtain boundless satisfaction. I have not written about these things with the intention of holding up a bogy-man to frighten the corrupt and mercenary children of the city, nor because I wish to prove that I as an artist am more exalted than they are. My sole purpose has been to point out the gospel contained in this state of affairs, and to invite all those who so desire to take advantage of it. Let me be more precise: the road which leads to the realm of poetry and art is open to everybody without exception. It is, I agree, pointless merely to count off on your fingers the years you have spent on this earth, and to pine for your lost youth. Nevertheless, by looking back over your life and reviewing all its various events in turn, you should be able to recall those times when, with heart aflame, you lost yourself in pure happiness. If you cannot do this, then you have nothing left to live for.

I do not say that pleasure for the poet lies in devoting him-self exclusively to one subject, or being transformed into just one thing. Sometimes he will become a solitary petal; some-times a pair of butterflies. He may even, like Wordsworth, become a host of daffodils: his heart brushed and set dancing by a gently rustling breeze. There are times, however, when he finds himself absorbed into his natural surroundings, with-out being aware of precisely what it is that has captured his heart. One man might explain the way he felt by saying that he had been mesmerized by the brilliance of Nature; another that it was as if he could hear the notes of an ethereal harp coming from somewhere deep within his soul. Yet another might describe his condition by saying that he seemed to be wandering on and on through a vast expanse, but getting nowhere because he was unfamiliar with the ground and everything there was incomprehensible to him. Everyone is at liberty to describe this condition any way that seems best to him. I was in just such a state of mind as, with my elbows resting on the ebony desk, I sat there gazing vacantly into space.

I was not thinking of anything, and I was certainly not looking at anything. Moreover, since nothing particularly striking had entered my field of consciousness, I could not be said to have been absorbed by anything either. I was, however, moving. It was not motion within the world, or even outside it; but for all that, I was moving. I was not going towards a particular flower or bird, nor against humanity. I was simply being carried along in a trance.

If pressed for an explanation, I would say that my soul was moving with the spring. Imagine all the colours, breezes, elements and voices of spring solidified, ground to powder and blended together to form an elixir of life, which had then been dissolved in dew gathered from the slopes of Olympus, and evaporated in the sun of fairyland. I felt now as though the vapour rising from just such a precious liquid had seeped through the pores of my skin and, without my being conscious of it, saturated my soul. The reason why the process of being assimilated into an object is pleasant is that it is usually accompanied by stimulation. In my case, however, this was not so, since it was impossible to say into what I had become assimilated. This absence of stimulation meant that I was filled with an indescribably profound and beautiful calm. Mine was no fleeting sense of wild elation like a wave raised momentarily by the wind only to subside again in an instant. No, the state I was in may best be likened to that of a vast ocean flowing across its unfathomable bed from continent to continent. The only difference is that I did not possess quite the same degree of vital energy as the ocean. This in fact was a good thing, for the manifestation of great vitality automatically gives rise to the anticipation of its exhaustion. Where it exists in a normal degree, however, there is no such worry. Not only had my soul become so faint that I seemed far removed from all anxiety as to whether or not my strength would some day drain from me, but it had also risen above its usual state of mediocrity. When I say that it had become faint, I do not mean to imply that it had grown weaker in any way, but simply that it had become more tenuous. I think the words 'nebulous' and 'limpid' which poets often use, describe this state admirably.

I wondered how it would be if I tried to express this condition on canvas, although I realised of course that it was not at all suitable material for a conventional picture. What the majority of people call a picture is nothing more than a direct reprint on silk of what the painter has seen around him, possibly after it has been filtered through an aesthetically critical eye. For them a picture has fulfilled its purpose if a flower looks like a flower, water reflects the light like water, and people behave as they do in real life. The only way the artist can create a painting which is not just simply run of the mill, is to bring his subject to life by giving it his own interpretation. No artist who tries to do this would consider that he had succeeded in producing a picture, unless his own personal viewpoint were apparent in every single brush stroke, for he is concerned with trying to highlight exactly what it is about the corner of Creation he is embracing that has inspired him.

Moreover, he would not make so bold as to claim that the picture were his own unless it clearly expressed his conviction, that although his opinions and perceptions owe nothing to those who have gone before, and are not governed by old traditions, yet nevertheless they are the most correct and the most beautiful.

However great the difference in depth of perception between these two types of artist may be, they have one thing in common: they both wait for some definite outside stimulus before putting brush to canvas. In my case, however, there was no such clearly defined subject. Although all my senses were on the alert, search as I might, I was unable to find in the objects around me any combination of shape, light and shade, strength and delicacy of line, and of course colour which was suitable for expressing how I felt. Since this feeling of mine had not come from without, or if it had, not from my visible surroundings, I could not point out any one thing as its source. Sometimes, as then, the feeling of inspiration exists by itself, independent of any material object, and my present problem was how I might express such a feeling as a picture. No, that is not strictly true: the real question was what object could I find which embodied it to such a degree that others looking at my painting would be able to feel as nearly as possible the way I was feeling at that moment.

All that is required to produce the average picture is something to paint. With the second type that I mentioned, however, it is necessary that the artist's feelings should be compatible with his subject. There is yet a third case in which he has to choose a subject which fits his inspiration. This is easier said than done, for very often even if he succeeds in selecting the components of his picture, he cannot cast them into any definite form. Let us suppose, however, that he does manage to produce such a form; the chances are that it will not be anything recognizable, and thus in the eyes of the general public it cannot be considered a picture. Even the artist himself will acknowledge that it does not represent anything which exists in the natural world. He will consider it a great achievement if he can convey a fraction of what he felt at the time he received his inspiration, and if he can bring that same unshakable tranquillity to even a few lives. I do not know whether anyone in the past has ever achieved this tremendous feat completely, but there are works in which the artist has had some degree of success. There are for example the paintings of bamboo by Wên T'ung, the landscapes of various types by the Unkoku school and by Ike Taiga, and the character sketches of Buson.[1] Since the vast majority of Western painters only take a fleeting glance at the substantial world, and are not at all concerned with matters which lie on such a refined and non-material plane, I should imagine that very few of them would be able to express so ethereal a sense on canvas.

It is unfortunate that the type of feeling which Sessyu[2] and Buson strove so hard to convey tends to be over simple, and is lacking in variety. From the point of view of technique, I could not of course hope to equal such great masters, yet the feeling I wished to depict was slightly more complex than theirs. It was this complexity which made it impossible for me to capture it completely within the bounds of a single picture. I now changed my position, and instead of resting my chin in my hands, continued to think with my arms folded on the desk. It made no difference; the ideas still would not come. You have to paint as though, in the instant when the right colours, shapes and mood all fell into place, your soul

[1] Wên T'ung—Chinese painter (1018-1079)
Unkoku Togan—Japanese landscape painter (1547-1618)
Ike Taiga—Japanese landscape painter (1723-1776)
Yosa Buson—Japanese painter and poet (1716-1783)
[2] Sessyu Toyo—Japanese painter (1420-1506)

suddenly became aware of its own existence. You must feel like a father who has searched the length and breadth of the land for his long lost child, with his purpose never out of his thoughts whether sleeping or waking, and who one day chances to meet him at some cross roads and cries instantly, 'Ah, here you are—at last!' This is a very difficult thing to do, but if I could do it, it would not matter to me what the people who saw my picture said about it. I would not be in the least upset even if they sneered and said it was not a picture at all. If something of what I felt were contained in the harmony of the colours; if I could breathe some of this power into the curve and sweep of the lines; if the overall tone of the picture spoke even fractionally of the pleasure I had experienced, then I would not care if the resulting shape were a cow, a horse, or somewhere between the two. No, I would not mind in the least, but somehow the ideas just would not come. I sat staring at my sketchbook until my eyes almost bored through the page. I schemed, and thought, and contrived, but it was no good: I could not give shape to my feelings.

I realised that it had been a mistake ever to try and turn such an abstract condition into a painting, and I put my pencil down. Since people are not all that different from one another, there must have been somebody, somewhere who had felt the same as I, and had tried to perpetuate his feelings by some means or other. Yes, but by what means I wondered.

Music! The word suddenly flashed into my mind. Of course! Music was the voice of Nature which, fathered by necessity, had been born in exactly such circumstances. I now became aware for the first time that music is something which must be listened to and learned. Unfortunately, however, I knew nothing whatsoever about this form of communication.

I thought next that I might possibly have some success with poetry, and so I stepped into the third realm. I seem to remember that Lessing argued that poetry can only be concerned with those events which are relevant to the passage of time, and thus established the fundamental principle that poetry and painting are two entirely different arts. Looked at in this light, it did not seem that poetry was suited to the mood which I had been so anxiously trying to express. Perhaps time was a contributory factor to the happiness which reached right down to the innermost depths of my soul. There was, however, no element in my present condition which had to follow the course of time and develop successively from one stage to another. My happiness was not due to the fact that one event arrived as another left, and was in turn followed by a third whose eventual departure heralded the birth of number four. It was derived from the atmosphere which pervaded my surroundings: an atmosphere of unvarying intensity which had remained with me there in that one place from the very beginning. It is those words 'remained in that one place' that are important, for they mean that even if I should try to translate this atmosphere into the common medium of language, there would be no necessity for the materials which had gone into creating it to be placed in any chronological order. All that would be necessary surely is that they be arranged specially as are the components of a picture. The problem was what features of my surroundings and what feelings should I use to represent this vast and vague state. I knew, however, that once having selected these, they would make admirable poetry—in spite of Lessing's contentions. However Homer and Virgil may have used poetry is beside the point. If you accept that it is suitable for expressing a mood, then it should be possible, providing that the simple special requirements of graphic art are fulfilled, to produce a verbal picture of that mood without making it the slave of time, and without the aid of events which follow each other in a regular progression.

Well that is enough of argument. I have forgotten most of *Laokoon*[1] and it is quite possible that if I read it through carefully I might find that I was on rather uncertain ground. Anyway, I had decided to try my hand at poetry since I had failed to produce a picture, and I sat rocking my body backwards and forwards, my pencil pressed firmly to the page. I tried and tried to make the point of that pencil move, but for some time I had no success whatsoever. Imagine that all at once you forget a friend's name. You feel that it is on the tip of your tongue, yet somehow it just will not come out. You know, however, that unless you keep on trying to remember, the name will slip back into the recesses of your mind. This is exactly the feeling one has when attempting to compose poetry. Let me take a more concrete example to illustrate the point. When you are making paste and first begin mixing the powder into the water, it presents not the slightest resistance to your chopsticks. Gradually, however, it starts to thicken, and the hand with which you are stirring feels a little heavy. You pay no attention to this, but continue until the mixture becomes so glutinous that you are scarcely able to stir any more. Finally the paste becomes so thick that it clings to the chopsticks, and they become bogged down.

My pencil moved fitfully on the page, but by persevering I succeeded in producing the following lines in about thirty minutes.

The months of spring are short as fleeting youth,
Yet sadness like the stems of fragrant plants is long.
Petals fall silently to earth in an empty garden,
And in the deserted hall a simple harp lies silent.

[1] This is the title of the work in which Lessing discussed the differences between poetry and painting.

Immobile in his web the spider hangs
As fingers of smoke trace round the bamboo beams.

On reading them through I had the impression that any one of these lines could have been turned into a picture. Why, I wondered, was it easier to write poetry than to paint. I thought that perhaps I should not have abandoned my attempt at painting, when with a little more effort I might have been successful. However, I had a desire to put into words a sentiment that could not be expressed on canvas. Once again I racked my brains, and eventually wrote:

Seated alone in silence undisturbed,
Within my heart a shaded light I see.
How futile the activity of man.
Oh, can I e'er forget this state
Where for one day tranquillity I find
And see how busy were the ages past for me?
Where can I lay this yearning soul to rest?
Far, far away among the milk-white clouds.

This time I read right from the beginning through all the lines I had written. I found them quite interesting, but considered as a description of my present ethereal state they definitely lacked something. I thought that I should have to continue my search, and decided while I was about it to write one more poem. As I sat there pencil in hand, I happened to glance towards the open doorway, and caught a glimpse of a beautiful shadowy form pass across the three foot space. 'Good heavens,' I thought.

By the time I had chanced to look up, this lovely figure was already half-hidden by the shōji which flanked the doorway. It had apparently been moving before I had noticed it, and now as I stared in amazement, it passed out of sight. I gave up all idea of writing poetry and fixed my gaze on the doorway.

In less than a minute the shadowy form reappeared from the opposite direction. It was the slender figure of a woman wearing a long-sleeved bridal gown. There was something forlorn about her as she walked noiselessly along the first floor verandah opposite. I let the forgotten pencil slip from my fingers, and suddenly caught my breath.

As so often happens in blossom time, a cloudy haze had gradually descended to deepen the dusk, bringing warning that at any moment it would rain. But over there, twelve yards away across the inner courtyard, the woman in the bridal gown continued her same graceful walk back and forth along the verandah. She had about her an air of serenity as she moved through the heavy air, her figure playing hide-and-seek among the evening shadows.

She said nothing, and looked neither to left nor right. So smoothly and quietly did she walk that not even her own ears could have caught the sound of her skirts trailing along the verandah. Her kimono from the waist down was covered with a bright design, but I was too far away to tell what it was. I could see, however, that the design and the plain background colour shaded gently together like the day and night whose border the woman herself was now treading.

I did not know why she had put on that gown with its long flowing sleeves, and was walking up and down the long passageway so persistently. Nor did I have any idea how long she had been at this unusual exercise dressed in such a totally unexpected way. Moreover, it was impossible to say in what, if anything, she was interested. However, it gave me a weird sensation to see this decorous and calm figure continually disappearing from view to reappear a moment later in the doorway, as she repeated her absolutely incomprehensible performance. She looked too unconcerned for this to be a lament at the passing of spring, and yet if

she was unconcerned, why was she arrayed in such beauti-
fully fine silk.

The colours of that late spring day were beginning to
deepen, and gave an unreal, dream-like tint to the world as it
lingered for a moment on the threshold of the long dark night.
Against this background the woman's strikingly beautiful obi,
which looked to me to be made of gold brocade, stood out in
vivid relief. Every few seconds, however, enveloped by the
dusky shades of evening, the bright material would vanish
into the void; only to appear a moment later in another place.
It was just like looking at a galaxy of brilliant stars which,
with the approach of dawn, fall back one by one into the
purple depths of the heavens.

As I watched the gates of night swing wide open to swallow
this bright and elegant figure into the lonely darkness, I felt
that there was a touch of the supernatural about the way in
which this woman, who, dressed as she was, should have been
the centre of attraction in a setting the visible world without
any apparent regret, and with no signs of trying to draw back.
Peering into the rapidly approaching gloom, I could see that
she was still calmly walking up and down the same stretch of
verandah at the same unhurried, even pace. She would, I
thought, have had to be extremely naive not to be aware of
the evil that was overtaking her. But it was uncanny if she was
aware of it and yet did not consider it an evil. If this were the
case, it meant that black was her natural home, and the reason
why she could stroll about so nonchalantly between existence
and non-existence was that this phantom shape which she had
temporarily assumed was now returning to the obscurity from
whence it had come. The way in which the pattern adorning
her gown merged with the unavoidable black surround
seemed to point to her origin.

At this point my thoughts turned on to another tack. Imag-
ine a beautiful girl who is apparently sleeping peacefully,

but who, without gaining consciousness at all, dies. How heartbreaking it would be for those sitting around the sickbed in such circumstances. If her pain had gradually become worse and worse until it had reached unbearable proportions, then not only would she herself have felt that life was not worth living, but her loved ones too might have reconciled themselves to the fact that death would be a merciful release. When, however, the child merely drifts into sleep and then dies, they wonder what they can possibly have done to deserve such a thing. To be carried off over the Styx like that without a chance to prepare oneself is, they think, tantamount to being tricked into a fatal ambush. If death must come, they would like to be forewarned so that they can resign themselves to the inevitable and pray for the soul of the dying girl. The chances are, however, that if they knew she were going to die before the actual event, they would not raise their voices to the Lord Buddha to ask him to receive this person who had already taken one step towards the next world, but would instead call out to the girl herself to make her return to them. To a person who is on the verge of slipping unawares from the sleep of this world into the sleep of eternity it may be painful to be called back, for it is merely adding one more strand to the rope of human passions which bound her to life, and which otherwise would soon have broken. She herself might say if she could, 'In the name of mercy, do not call me. Let me sleep in peace.' Nevertheless they would still want to call her.

I thought that the next time I saw the woman through the doorway, I might call out to her to rouse her from the coma into which she had fallen. No sooner had the shadow glided like a dream back into view, however, than my tongue seemed to cleave to the roof of my mouth. I made up my mind that the next time I would call without fail, but again I could not. As I was trying to work out why it was that I was unable to say anything, the woman passed by yet again. It was obvious that she had not the slightest idea that there was somebody over here who kept watching for her, and who was worrying about her so anxiously. It irked me the way she seemed to consider it beneath her dignity to notice such a person as I. I was still saying, 'Next time, next time' to myself, when the layer of clouds, as if unable to hold back any longer, let fall a melancholy screen of fine rain which completely hid the figure from sight.

✦ 7 ✦

Brrr! It was cold. Towel in hand, I went down for a warm bath. I undressed in a small matted room, and then went down the four steps into the bathroom which was about twelve feet square. There appeared to be no shortage of stones in these parts, for both the floor, and the lining of the sunken bath tank in the centre were of pebbles set in cement. The tank was about the size of the vats they used to make bean-curd, being roughly four feet deep. This place was called a mineral spring, so there were presumably many mineral ingredients in the water. As, in spite of this, it was clear and transparent, I found it very pleasant to bathe in. From time to time some of the water found its way into my mouth, but it had no distinctive taste or odour. This spring was said to have medical properties, but I never took the trouble to find out what ailments it was supposed to cure. Since I myself was not suffering from any illness, the idea that the spring might have any practical value did not enter my head. As I stepped into the tank all I was thinking of was a poem by the Chinese poet Pai Le-tien that expresses the feeling of pleasure which the mere mention of the words 'hot spring' rouses in me.

The waters of the spring caress;
And smooth away all coarseness from my skin.

All that I ask of any hot spring is that it give me just such a pleasant feeling, but if it is unable to do so, in my opinion it is worthless.

The water came up to my chest, and I stood there soaking myself thoroughly. I do not know from where the hot water gushed, but it was constantly pouring over the sides in an attractive stream. I was happy, and very much at ease as there in the springtime I felt beneath my feet the warmth of those stones which were never dry. So gentle and quiet was the falling rain that it was able to dampen the spring without the night being aware of it, and yet clusters of raindrops had gradually formed on the eaves, and now their rhythmic 'drip, drip' as they fell to earth reached my ears. The steam which completely filled the room from floor to ceiling was so confined that it escaped wherever it could find a crack or even a tiny knot-hole.

The cold mists of autumn; the tranquil haze which hangs over the world in spring; the blue smoke rising from cooking fires at evening; all these are capable of drawing my ephemeral form up with them into the limitless expanse of the heavens. Yes, there are many things which can charm me, and whose cry finds an answering echo within me; but only on a spring evening, with my body softly enveloped in clouds of steam from a hot bath, can I feel that I belong to a bygone age. The steam which draped itself around me was not so dense that I was unable to see. Nor yet was it as thin as a layer of sheer silk which may easily be torn aside to reveal the ordinary mortal figure beneath. I was isolated in a warm rainbow: shut in on all sides by steam from which I could never emerge however many layers I might pull aside. One can talk of becoming drunk on wine, but I have never heard the phrase 'to become drunk on vapour'. Even if there were such a phrase, it could not of course be used of mist, and is rather too strong to use of haze. Nevertheless it does become apt when used to describe the steam rising from a hot bath, but then only in the context of a spring evening.

Leaning my head back against the side of the tank, I let my weightless body rise up through the hot water to the point of least resistance. As I did so I felt my soul to be floating like a jelly-fish. The world is an easy place to live in when you feel like this. You throw off the shackles of common sense, and break through the bars of desire and physical attachment. Lying in the hot water, you allow it to do with you as it likes, and become absorbed into it. The more freely you are able to float, the easier life becomes, until if your very soul floats, you will be in a state more blessed than had you become a disciple of Christ. Following this train of thought, even the idea of drowning is not without a certain refinement and elegance. I believe it was Swinburne who, in one or other of his poems, described a drowned woman's feeling of joy at having attained eternal peace. Looked at in this light, Millais' 'Ophelia', which has always had a disturbing effect on me, becomes a thing of considerable beauty. It had been a constant puzzle to me why he had chosen to paint such an unhappy scene, but I now realised that it was after all a good subject for a picture. There is certainly something aesthetic in the sight of a figure being carried along by the current free from all pain, whether it be floating, beneath the surface, or rising and sinking by turns. Moreover, it will undoubtedly make an excellent picture if both banks are decked with many kinds of flowers whose colours blend unobtrusively with those of the water, the person's clothes and her complexion. If the facial expression is perfectly peaceful the picture becomes almost mythical or allegorical. A look of convulsive agony will destroy the whole mood, while one which is absolutely composed and devoid of all passion will fail to convey any of the girl's emotions. What expression ought one portray to be successful? It may well be that Millais' 'Ophelia' is a success, but I doubt whether he and I are of the same mind. Still, Millais is Millais, and I am myself; and I wanted to express the aesthetic quality of drowning according to my own convictions. It seemed, however, that it was going to be a difficult task to find the face I wanted.

Still floating in the bath, I composed the following eulogy on drowning.

Beneath the earth where all is black as night,
The drenching rain seeps down
And frost descends to chill;
But in spring water,
Buoyed by waves or lying in the deep,
There is no pain.

As I lay there absently murmuring the lines over to myself, I heard the sound of a samisen. Although I am supposed to be an artist, I am ashamed to say that in fact such knowledge as I have about this instrument is decidedly unsound. My ear would never detect anything unusual even if the second string were sharp or the third flat. Nevertheless, in that small mountain village on a spring night, to which even the rain lent an added sense of pleasure, it was delightful to listen idly to the distant strains of a samisen as I floated body and soul in the hot water. It was too far away for me to be able to recognise either the words or the tune of what was being played, and this gave the music a certain charm. Judging from the mellow tone, I thought the instrument might be one of the thicker-necked samisens which, I believe, the blind minstrals of the Kyoto area used to accompany folk songs.

When I was a boy there was a wine shop called Yorozuya just beyond the gate of our house, and on quiet spring afternoons the proprietor's young daughter, O-Kura, would always practise singing and playing long epic ballads. As soon as she began, I would go into the garden to listen to her. Just in front of our tea-garden, which was a little over forty square yards in size, three pine trees stood in a row along the eastern side of the guest rooms. They were tall trees with trunks about a foot in circumference, but the interesting thing was that they only looked elegant when viewed as a group. As a child, I remember, it gave me a great deal of pleasure to look at these trees. Beneath the three pines, there was a slab of some kind of reddish rock on which stood a metal lantern blackened and rusted with age. It was always there like some cantankerous and obstinate old man who refused to budge, and I used to love to sit and gaze at it. Around the lantern wild spring flowers and tall grasses whose names I did not know pushed through the thickly moss-covered ground. They appeared to pay no attention to the changing world about them, nor to fear the wind that might destroy them. Alone they gave off their fragrance, and alone they were happy. I used to seek out a small space where I could kneel among the flowers without crushing them, and there I would crouch quietly. To gaze at the lantern beneath the pine trees, to smell the perfume of the flowers and to listen to the sound of O-Kura playing and singing ballads in the distance became my daily routine.

O-Kura would have left behind her long ago the age when she wore red silk ribbons in her hair, and now probably presented a rather dowdy domesticated picture as she served behind the shop counter. I wondered whether she was happily married, and whether the swallows still looked as busy as ever, carrying in their beaks mud for their nests. Somehow I just could not get those swallows and the smell of rice-wine out of my head.

Were the three pine trees still standing there as elegantly as before? The metal lantern would doubtless be broken. Did the spring flowers remember a small boy who knelt among them? No, even in those days they had gone their own sweet way without a word, so there was no reason why they should remember now. Nor would they have retained the memory of O-Kura's voice as every day she sang: 'The hempen gown of the wandering priest . . .'

At the sound of the samisen, this unexpected panorama had opened up before me, and I found myself in the mysterious and wonderful world of the past. Once again I was that small boy who had lived twenty years ago. Suddenly the door of the bathroom slid open. 'Somebody has come in,' I thought, and without changing my position I raised my eyes towards the door. Since I was lying with my head resting on the side farthest away from the door, I was able to see the steps which led down to the bath, diagonally opposite to me and approximately twenty feet away. As yet, however, no one had come into view. For a while the only sound was of raindrops falling from all around the eaves, for the samisen had stopped playing at some time or other.

At length something appeared at the head of the steps. Although large, the room was lit only by one small hanging lantern, and so even had the air been completely clear, it would still have been difficult to distinguish anything accurately at this distance. To make matters worse, however, this evening the rising steam was unable to escape, being shut into the bathroom by the fine drizzle outside, and it became absolutely impossible to tell who was standing there. Whoever it was put one foot down on to the second step, but as at that moment the light was not falling directly on them, I could not make out whether it was a man or a woman, and was thus at a loss what to say.

The dark shape descended to the next step without a sound, making it seem that the stone underfoot was as soft as velvet. Indeed, anyone judging from the sound would have been excused for thinking that there had been no movement at all. The shimmering outline had now become a little more clearly discernible. Being an artist, I have an unusually good sense of perception concerning the structure of the human body, and no sooner had this unknown person moved down a step than I realised that I was alone in the bathroom with a woman.

I was still floating there, trying to decide whether or not to give any indication of having seen her, when quite suddenly and without any reserve she appeared directly before me. She stood there surrounded by swirling eddies of mist into which the gentle light suffused a rose-tinted warmth, and the sight of her lithe and upright figure, crowned with billowing clouds of jet-black hair, drove all thoughts of good manners, civility and propriety out of my head. My whole being was filled with the realisation that I had discovered a beautiful artistic subject.

I have no complaint to make against classical Greek sculpture, but whenever I see one of those nude paintings which seem to have become the lifeblood of contemporary French art, I feel that somehow it is lacking in refinement, for it is obvious that the artist has gone to extremes to express the beauty of uncovered flesh. I cannot say that such paintings have ever perturbed me unduly, but I have, from time to time, been annoyed at my inability to define why I thought them indelicate. I know that in covering up the human body one is concealing a thing of beauty, and yet to leave it uncovered makes it common. The modern painters of nudes are not even content with reproducing as it is the body they have deprived of attire, but thrust it to a nauseating extent on to the clothed world round about. They forgot that it is a natural thing for man to wear clothes, and attempt to give nudity all the rights. Instead of leaving well alone, they try with all their might to get the nakedness to scream out to you from the canvas. When art is carried to such lengths it debases itself by coercing the people who look at it. If you struggle to make a thing of perfect beauty appear more beautiful, you will only succeed in detracting from it. This idea is expressed, with regard to everyday life, in the proverb: 'From Perfection there is only one road—down.'

Placidity and simplicity both indicate the presence of that underlying depth which is an indispensible ingredient of art and literature. The shortcomings of modern art may be attributed to the way in which the so-called tide of civilisation is indiscriminately sweeping aside the 'old guard' in its impatient haste to advance. Nude paintings provide a good example of this. In the cities we have Geisha, those women who trade on their physical charms, and to whom the art of flattery is a means of earning a living. When they are with a 'client', their sole expression is one of anxiously trying to impress him with their appearance. The nude beauties who fill the perennial salon catalogues to overflowing are similar to these Geisha. Not only are they unable to forget their own nakedness, but they use to the uttermost every muscle in their bodies to make the viewer aware of it.

There was, however, no trace of any such vulgarity about the exquisite form before me. As soon as you use the words 'stripped of clothes', you have already descended to the level of ordinary mortals; but this woman looked as natural as if she had been conjured up in a cloud in the age of the gods, before there were any clothes to cover the body or any sleeves to put arms through.

Wave upon wave of steam rolled upwards refracting and diffusing the late spring light, and filling the entire room with a warmly scintillating rainbow. There in the opalescent depths rose her pure white form, gradually shading into hair so dimly visible as to make it difficult to determine whether indeed it was black or not. What a superb figure.

The line of her neck on both sides turned lightly inwards, and then sloping easily downwards, rounded the ample shoulders and flowed on down her arms, separating at the ends to form the fingers. Beneath the two well-formed breasts the wave of her body subsided for a while to rise again gently as the firm full line of her abdomen. This fullness receded in its turn, and faded at the line of her groin. From here the thigh muscles stood out slightly, being tensed to preserve her balance. The long sweeping undulation of her leg was deflected by the knee and sent curving down to the heel. Here the whole intricacy of line was resolved and carried finally to the sole of her tapering foot. Such complexity yet unity of structure was surely unique. It would be impossible to find a shape so natural, so soft, so lacking in resistance and yet so unobtrusive.

It was not in fact thrust flagrantly into view like the average nude, but being only dimly visible in the midst of a strange aura of enchantment which lent mystery to all within it, gave no more than a subtle hint of its full beauty. There was about it that same artistically perfect combination of atmosphere, warmth and sense of the ethereal that exists in a picture in which the artist suggests the presence of a horned dragon merely by dotting a few scales here and there in an inky black haze. If it is true that a dragon on which every single scale has been carefully painted looks ludicrous, then conversely the naked human body when looked at with deference retains its sublime loveliness. When I first caught sight of this figure I thought it might be some beautiful maiden who had fled down to earth from the kingdom of the moon, and who now stood there hesitating, surrounded by the rainbow which had pursued her.

The whiteness of the woman's skin came floating towards me, and I feared that with one more step my maiden from the moon would degenerate into a being of this common world. Just then, however, her thick blue-black hair streamed around her with a swish like the tail of some gigantic legendary turtle cleaving through the waves. Next moment her white figure was flying up the steps tearing through the veils of mist. A clear peal of feminine laughter rang out in the corridor and gradually echoed away into the distance, leaving the bathroom quiet again. The water washed over my face, so I stood up. As I did so, startled waves lapped against my chest, and splashed noisily over the sides of the tank.

✦ 8 ✦

I had been invited to have tea with old Mr. Shioda. Besides myself, the other guests were Daitetsu the abbot of the Kankaiji temple, and a young layman who was about twenty-four or twenty-five years of age. To get from my room to the old man's I just had to go down the passage to the right, and turn left at the end. His room was about twelve feet long by nine feet wide, but seemed smaller because of the large rose-wood table set in the centre. Looking towards the place he had indicated I should sit, I noticed instead of a cushion, there was a beautiful rug spread there, which was obviously Chinese. Strange and wonderful houses and willow trees had been woven into a hexagon in the middle, and the surround was an almost metallic shade of indigo. In each of the four corners was a pattern of brown rings interwoven with a creeper-like design. I doubt whether such a rug would ever be used in a Chinese sitting-room, but it looked very nice as a substitute for a cushion. Just as the merit of Indian chintz and Persian tapestry lies in their conservatism, so the charm of this rug lay in its lack of frivolous detail. This lack is not only noticeable in Chinese carpets, but in all their furniture and ornaments. Looking at them, you cannot fail to realise that they were created by a stolid, patient people. What makes these objects so superlative is their ability to absorb one's interest utterly and completely. Japan produces her works of art with the attitude of a pick-pocket, while in the West everything must be on a grand scale, and is inseparable from the material world. It was with these thoughts in mind that I took my seat. The young man sat down next to me, occupying half the rug.

The abbot was seated on a tiger skin whose tail stretched out near my knees and whose head was underneath our host. Mr. Shioda was completely bald, but had a bushy white beard, giving the impression that the hair had been transplanted from his head to his face. He now placed the teacups on their saucers and carefully arranged them on the low table. Turning to the abbot he said: 'How are you? It's been quite a time since we had a guest, so I thought it would be nice if we all had some tea together.'

'Thank you for the invitation,' replied the abbot. 'I was only thinking today that it had been so long since I had been to see you, that I really would have to call in.' He was a man of about sixty, whose once round face had now collapsed into the mellow lines of age. In fact he looked for all the world like a picture of Dharma Buddha which someone had sketched with rapid unsteady strokes. He seemed to have been a close friend of Mr. Shioda's for a long time.

'I presume this gentleman is the guest you were speaking of,' he continued.

Nodding his head in assent, Mr. Shioda tilted the small vermilion teapot and allowed a few precious drops of the green-tinged amber liquid to trickle into each of the cups. I could feel the delicate aroma gently assailing my nostrils.

'You probably find it rather lonely right out here in the country by yourself, don't you?' the abbot asked me as soon as the tea had been poured.

For reply I made as non-committal a noise as possible. To say that I was lonely would have been untrue, and yet if I said I was not, it would necessitate giving a long explanation.

'No, Abbot,' broke in Mr. Shioda, 'this gentleman has come here to paint, so he has plenty to do.'

'Oh really? That's splendid. I suppose you belong to the Nansō school.'

This time I answered with a plain 'No'. I felt sure the abbot would not have understood if I had said that I painted in the Western style.

'No, he paints in that Western style.' Once again Mr. Shioda, in his role as host, had taken upon himself the task of answering for me.

'Oh, the Western style? Then you must paint the same sort of things as Kyuichi here. I saw one of his pictures for the first time the other day, and I must say it was very pretty.'

'Oh no, it wasn't any good at all,' protested the young man, speaking at last.

'Did you show one of your paintings to the abbot then?' Mr. Shioda asked him. Judging from the way he spoke and from his attitude, I thought they might be related.

'Well, I didn't exactly show it to him; he just happened to catch me painting down by the Kagami pond.'

'Hm. Did he now?—Well, the tea's poured out, so please start.' So saying he placed a cup before each of us. Although the cup itself was large, there was only a very small amount of tea in the bottom. The dark grey exterior of the cup was covered with deep red and pale yellow brush strokes, but whether these were meant to form a picture, a pattern or a devil's mask motif I could not imagine.

'It's by Mokubei,' explained old Mr. Shioda simply.

'It's very interesting,' I replied with equal brevity.

'There seem to be a lot of imitations about—have a look at the bottom, the name's written there.'

I picked it up, and in order to see better turned towards the shōji on which were thrown the warm elliptical shadows of the leaves of a 'haran' plant standing in a pot outside.

Bending my head forward I peeped inside the cup, and there sure enough was the name 'Mokubei' in small letters. I do not think the name is particularly important as far as the appreciation of an object is concerned, and yet apparently it is something which collectors set great store by. Instead of putting the cup back down on the table, I raised it to my lips.

For the man of leisure there is no more refined nor delightful pursuit than savouring this thick delicious nectar drop by drop on the tip of the tongue. The average person talks of 'drinking' tea, but this is a mistake. Once you have felt a little of the pure liquid spread slowly over your tongue, there is scarcely any need to swallow it. It is merely a question of letting the fragrance penetrate from your throat right down to your stomach. On no account should it be swilled round the mouth and over the teeth, for this is extremely coarse. 'Gyokuro' tea escapes the insipidity of pure water and yet is not so thick as to require any tiring jaw action. It is a wonderful beverage. Some complain that if they drink tea they cannot sleep, but to them I would say that it is better to go without sleep than without tea.

While I was engrossed in these thoughts, Mr. Shioda had brought out a cake bowl which was the colour of sapphires. The skill and precision with which the craftsman had shaved away large lumps of the porcelain to leave parts of the wall so thin as to be translucent was truly amazing. When I held it up to the light, it seemed as though the spring shadows had darted into the bowl, and then become trapped having forgotten the way out. I was glad that it was empty.

'I heard how you admired celadon porcelain, so I thought I would show you a little today.'

'What celadon porcelain is that you're talking about?' broke in the abbot. 'Oh, the cake bowl. Yes, I like that too. By the way,' he went on to me, 'do you think it would be possible to paint a Western style picture on a fusuma[1]? If it would, I'd like to ask you to do one for me.'

I could hardly refuse outright, but I was not sure whether the abbot would like my painting. It would, I felt, have been a great pity if I spent a considerable amount of effort on it, only to have him say that he did not care for the Western style of painting; so I said, 'I don't think it would go well on a fusuma.'

'No, perhaps it wouldn't. If Kyuichi's picture which I saw the other day is anything to go by, it might be a little too gaudy.'

'Oh, mine was no good, I was only messing about,' said the young man modestly, obviously acutely embarrassed.

'Where is that what's-its-name pond you mentioned just now?' I asked him out of curiosity.

'It's in a secluded spot down in the valley behind the Kankaiji temple—it was only that I learned a little Western painting when I was at school, so I thought I'd go down there to while away the time.'

'The Kankaiji temple?'

'That's where I am,' the abbot answered. 'It's a nice place. It looks right down on the sea, and—well, you must come and see for yourself while you're here; it's not half a mile away. Look, you can see the stone steps that lead up to the temple, from the verandah there.'

'May I really come up and visit you sometime?'

'Yes, of course. I'm always there. Mr. Shioda's daughter often comes.—Speaking of O-Nami, I haven't seen her today.—Is there anything wrong with her, Mr. Shioda?'

'She's probably gone out somewhere. I don't suppose she went to your place Kyuichi, did she?'

'No, I didn't see her.'

'I expect she's gone off on one of her lone walks again,'

[1] An opaque, paper-covered sliding door or screen.

put in the abbot. 'Ha, ha, ha. She certainly has a sturdy pair of legs. I had to go down to Tonami the other day on a clerical matter, and when I got near Sugatami bridge I saw someone that I thought looked remarkably like O-Nami. Sure enough, when I got closer I found it was her. There she was with her kimono tucked right up at the back, and wearing a pair of straw sandals. Well, she suddenly turned to me, and burst out with, "Hello, Abbot. What are you standing there gaping for? Where are you going?" It quite took me aback, I can tell you. Ha, ha, ha, ha. When I asked her where on earth she'd been, dressed like that, she said that she'd been gathering parsley. And then she said, "I'll give you some, Abbot," and without more ado she thrust a bunch of the muddy parsley into my sleeve. Ha, ha, ha, ha, ha.'

'Did she really? I . . . .' said the girl's father with a sickly grin. He then turned the conversation sharply back to curios with: 'I'd like you to have a look at this.'

The old damask silk bag which he had just taken down from a rosewood book-shelf appeared to contain something quite heavy.

'Have you ever seen this, Abbot?'

'What on earth is it?'

'An ink-stone.[1]'

'Oh, really. What kind of an ink-stone?'

'Well, it is said to have been a prized possession of the calligrapher Sanyo, and . . . .'

'No, I've never seen it.'

'The spare lid was decorated by Shunsui, and . . . .'

'No, I don't think I've ever seen it. Come on, hurry up.'

With an air of great importance Mr. Shioda untied the string at the neck of the damask bag, exposing one corner of a red oblong stone.

[1] A stone on which a solid stick of ink is rubbed down and mixed with water.

'It's a lovely colour, isn't it?' remarked the abbot. 'Is it "Tankei" stone?'

'Oh yes, of course. It's of excellent quality, and it has "bird's-eye" markings in the grain.—Nine of them.'

'Nine!' The abbot appeared very impressed.

'And this is the spare lid which was decorated by Shunsui,' went on the old man, taking out a thin lid from its figured satin wrapping. On it was written a Chinese poem of seven characters in Shunsui's handwriting.

'Ah yes. Shunsui has a nice hand; a very nice hand. But I think that Kyohei was the better calligrapher.'

'I think that the least skilful of all was Sanyo. There's no doubt he was a genius, but I find his writing singularly uninteresting.'

'Ha, ha, ha. I know how much you dislike Sanyo's writing, Abbot, so I've taken his scroll down from the wall for today, and put another one up in its place.'

'Oh, have you?' said the abbot, turning round to look at the alcove behind him where the scroll usually hung. In the alcove was a low wooden dais which had been polished until it shone like a mirror. On this stood an old tarnished copper vase in which magnolia sprays about two feet high had been arranged. The present scroll was by the Chinese calligrapher Wu Tsu-lai, and around the edges was the dark lustre of gold brocade with which it had been carefully bound. The scroll itself was not of silk but paper. The passage of time, however, had matched the colour of the paper with that of the cloth on which it was mounted, giving to the whole a harmony which was independent of the writing it contained. I felt sure that the gold brocade too had not possessed its present dignity when it had first been woven, for now the colours had faded, and the gold thread frayed. The more gorgeous parts had become obliterated, making the sober portions more prominent. The ivory rod from which the scroll was suspended could be seen protruding from both sides, its whiteness standing out in sharp relief against the dark red of the wall. In spite of this splash of colour, and the magnolias which appeared to be floating there lightly in space, the whole alcove seemed very dull, even gloomy.

Still looking at the scroll the abbot said, 'It's by Tsu-lai, isn't it?'

'Yes. I wasn't sure whether you liked his work very much either, but I thought at least he would be better than Sanyo.'

'He's far and away the better calligrapher. The Japanese scholars who lived when Yoshimune was Shogun[1] copied everything Chinese slavishly, and their writing wasn't very good. But for all that, you know, there is a certain quality about it.'

'Wasn't it Tsu-lai who said that generally speaking the Japanese were better calligraphers than the Chinese?'

'I don't know. I don't think they were as good as all that. Ha, ha, ha, ha, ha.'

'By the way, Abbot, who did you learn calligraphy from?'

'Me? Why, Zen priests don't go in for reading and writing you know.'

'No, but who did you learn from?'

'I studied Takaizumi's writing a little when I was young, that's all. But I'm always willing to write something if anyone asks me to. Ha, ha, ha. By the way,' he urged, 'how about showing us that ink-stone.'

All eyes now turned to the ink-stone as it was very slowly drawn out of the damask bag. It was about twice the usual thickness, measuring roughly two inches, and it was approximately four inches wide by six inches long, which is the average size. On the lid, which was of pine-bark polished in its natural rough state, were two unreadable Chinese characters written in red lacquer.

---

[1] Tokugawa Yoshimune was Shōgun (military leader) of Japan from 1716 to 1735.

'This lid,' began the old man, 'this lid is no ordinary one, and so as you can see, although it is undeniably of pine-bark . . .' So saying he let his eyes rest on me. As an artist, however, I felt unable to enthuse about the origin and history of a pine-bark lid, so I said, 'I think a pine lid is rather common, don't you?'

Mr. Shioda raised his hands in a horrified gesture, and seemed on the point of saying, 'Good gracious!' Instead he replied, 'If it were just any old pine lid, it might be common I agree, but this one was made by Sanyo himself from bark that he stripped from a pine tree in the garden when he was in Hiroshima.'

Thinking that, as I had suspected, Sanyo had been a man of little taste, I said, 'Now I know that it was made by Sanyo himself, it seems even more clumsy than before. I feel that it would have been better had he left the rough bark alone, and not polished it like that.'

Hereupon the abbot let out a loud guffaw, and came to my support by saying, 'You're absolutely right; it makes the lid look cheap and tawdry.'

The young man looked pityingly at old Mr. Shioda's face. Mr. Shioda himself pushed the lid sullenly to one side, thus revealing the true shape of the ink-stone underneath.

The most striking and attractive thing about the stone was the figure which had been carved on the upper surface. In the middle, a lump of the stone had been left slightly raised up in relief, and this was in the form of a spider's body. Radiating from the body were the eight legs, each of which ended at one of the 'bird's-eye' markings. The remaining 'bird's-eye' was in the centre of the body, and gave the impression that a drop of yellow juice had been spilled there and then smudged. A channel about an inch deep had been gouged out around the perimeter, beyond the compass of the legs. Surely, I thought, one was not supposed to mix the ink in there, for it looked as though it would hold over a quarter of a pint of water. Presumably one took a drop of water from the container with a small silver spoon, poured it on to the spider's back, and there ground down a little of the precious ink tablet. If this were not so, then in spite of its name the ink-stone was really no more than a desk ornament.

The old man opened his mouth to speak, and looked as though at any moment he were going to dribble. 'Look at the arrangement and the markings. They're beautiful.'

He was quite right. The more one looked, the more attractive the colours became. I could imagine breathing on the cold surface, and watching the breath absorbed and turned into a mist which would permeate the richness of the colour beneath. The most remarkable thing was the colour of the 'eyes', or rather the almost imperceptible way in which their colour gradually merged and blended with the surround, throwing one's vision out of focus. When I readjusted my gaze, the 'eyes' looked as though they were right down in the transparent depths, like black beans set in a mauve-coloured jelly. An ink-stone which has even one or two of these 'bird's-eyes' is rare, and there are scarcely any at all which have nine. Should all these markings be spread equidistantly, then to think that the stone has been artificially made, is to commit a gross and unpardonable slander against one of Nature's greatest rarities.

'Yes, it certainly is wonderful. Not only is it pleasant to look at but it feels nice too,' I said, passing the ink-stone to the young man next to me.

'Do you understand such things, Kyuichi?' asked the old man with a laugh.

'No, I don't!' replied Kyuichi, flinging the words out roughly. He then passed the incomprehensible ink-stone back to me, as if he thought it a waste for him to be gazing at it. After I had turned it round once more, carefully feeling the pleasant surface beneath my fingers, I handed it on politely to the abbot. He placed it on the palm of his hand and stared at it for a time, and then as though this did not satisfy him, he polished the back of the spider on his brown cotton robe in the most inexcusable fashion, and once again gazed with admiration at its lustre.

'You know, Mr. Shioda,' he said, 'this really does have a lovely colour. Have you ever used it?'

'No. If anything happened to it, it could never be replaced, so I've kept it just the same as the day I bought it.'

'Yes, I expect this type of ink-stone is rare even in China.'

'Yes indeed.'

'I'd very much like one too. Perhaps I'll ask Kyuichi to get one for me. How about it Kyuichi; will you bring one back with you?'

'I'll probably be killed before I have a chance to find one,' laughed the young man.

'Oh, I was forgetting. This is no time to be talking of ink-stones. When do you leave?'

'Within the next two or three days.'

'Are you going down to Yoshida to see him off, Mr. Shioda?'

'Well, I'm getting old, and in the normal way I would just say good-bye here. But since I don't know whether I'll ever see him again, I have decided to go.'

'You don't have to go to all that trouble, uncle,' Kyuichi said. Apparently then he was the old man's nephew. Now I came to think about it, there was a resemblance between them.

'Let your uncle come and see you off,' put in the abbot. 'There's no reason why he shouldn't if he goes downriver by boat, is there, Mr. Shioda?'

'No. It would be very difficult if I had to cross the mountains, but by boat, even though it is a long way . . . .'

This time the young man kept silent and raised no objection.

'Are you off to China then?' I asked him.

'Yes.'

Although I felt this monosyllable to be scarcely an adequate answer, I had no reason to pry into his affairs, so I let the matter rest. I looked at the shōji and noticed that the 'haran' leaves had moved.

'Kyuichi! What are you thinking of?—He's been called up to go to the war because he was with the volunteers before.'

The old man went on to explain to me that his nephew would have to leave very soon for the Manchurian plains.

Since my arrival I had been under the impression that this was an idyllic dream-like mountain village where birds sang, petals fell to the earth and hot water gushed forth in streams, but where nothing else ever happened. How wrong I had been, for Reality had crossed the seas and mountains to this isolated old village to call again to battle the descendants of that once mighty clan, the Taira, the warriors of Mediaeval days. The time might now come when this young man's blood would trickle from his veins to be lost in a greater crimson tide that would stain the bleak and barren plains of Manchuria. Or possibly the time might come when from the point of the long sword he had buckled on, he himself would send another rivulet to join the tide, and another soul wafting upwards like a wisp of smoke. Yet here he sat now, next to a painter for whom dreaming was the only thing of value that life had to offer. He sat so close that had that painter listened carefully he could have even heard the beat of the young man's heart—a beat in which perhaps already were echoes of a rising tide rolling across a plain hundreds of miles away. Fate had brought these two together under the same roof, and then had left without a word.

✦ 9 ✦

'Are you studying?' asked a woman's voice. I had come back to my own room, and was reading one of the books which I had brought along on the trip tied to my tripod.

'Come in. You're not disturbing me at all.'

Without any further preamble the woman walked boldly into the room. Her well-shaped neck rose gracefully from the neck-band of her kimono, and the first thing that caught my attention as she knelt down in front of me was the contrast between the pallor of her neck and the subdued colour of the neck-band.

'I see you're reading a foreign book. I expect it's all about the most complicated things, isn't it?'

'Not really.'

'Well then, what is it about?'

'That's a difficult question. To tell you the truth I'm not absolutely sure myself.'

'Ha, ha, ha. And you call that study?'

'It isn't meant to be study. I just lay the book open on the desk, and pick out passages to read at random.'

'Do you enjoy that?'

'Yes, I enjoy it.'

'Why?'

'Why? Well, because that's the most interesting way to read a novel.'

'What a strange person you are to be sure.'

'Yes, I suppose I am a little odd.'

'What's wrong with reading a novel from the beginning?'

'Because if you start reading from the beginning, you have to go on to the end.'

'That seems a peculiar reason. What's wrong with reading to the end?'

'Nothing at all, naturally. I do it myself when I want to read the story.'

'But if you don't read the story, what else is there left?'

'Yes, she's a woman all right,' I thought, and decided to test her a little.

'Do you like novels?'

'Me?'—a pause, and then, 'Well—you know,' she added vaguely. Apparently not very much.

'You don't know yourself one way or the other, do you?'

'I don't really mind whether I read them or not,' she said in a voice which suggested that in her eyes novels had no claim to existence.

'If that's the case, surely it doesn't matter whether you start from the beginning, from the end, or pick out odd pieces here and there. I can't see why you find my way of reading so curious.'

'Ah, but you and I are different.'

'How?' I asked, looking deep into her eyes. Her gaze, however, did not waver for an instant, which made me feel that it was I who was being examined.

'Ha, ha, ha. You mean you don't know?'

At this I stopped my frontal attack and decided to try a flanking movement. 'But surely you must have read quite a bit when you were young.'

'I still consider myself to be young even now, you unkind man.' Yet again the hawk I sent up missed its prey. The woman was constantly on her guard.

'If you can say that in front of a man, you must be getting

on in years,' I remarked, returning with some difficulty to press my original attack.

'You must be quite old yourself if you have enough experience to make such a statement. Are you still interested in the flights and frolics of love at your age?'

'Yes, very. I shall be interested in them as long as I live.'

'Really? I suppose that is what makes you an artist.'

'Exactly. And because I am an artist I find any passage of a novel interesting even when it is out of context. I find it interesting talking to you—so much so in fact that I'd like to talk to you every day while I'm here. I'll even fall in love with you if you like; that would be particularly interesting. But however deeply I were to fall in love with you it would not mean that we had to get married. If you think that marriage is the logical conclusion to falling in love, then it becomes necessary to read novels through from beginning to end.'

'What an inhuman way of falling in love you artists have.'

'Not "*in*human"; *non*-human. It is because we read novels with this same non-human, objective approach that we don't care about the plot. For us it is interesting to flip open the book as impartially as if we were drawing a sacred lot, and to read aimlessly at wherever it falls open.'

'Hm, it does sound interesting, I agree. Tell me a little about the passage you were just reading. I want to know where its interest lies.'

'It's no good telling you about it. A painting isn't worth a brass farthing if you just describe it to someone, is it?'

'Ha, ha, ha. Well, read it to me.'

'In English, you mean?'

'No, in Japanese.'

'It will be a job to read English as Japanese.'

'That's all right; it will give you the right feeling of detachment.'

I thought that this might be amusing for a little, so I consented to her request. Very slowly and hesitantly I began to translate the part of the book I had been reading into Japanese. If there is such a thing as an objective way of reading, then mine was certainly it. The woman too seemed to be listening in a completely detached manner.

'"Waves of tender emotion radiated from the woman—from her voice, from her eyes and from her skin. Helped by the man she went aft. Did she go to look at Venice in the dusk, and did the man give her his hand to set the lightning coursing through his veins?"—Since I'm being objective about this, I'm just giving you the gist of what is written. I may leave out some parts.'

'That doesn't matter at all. I don't even mind if you put in some things of your own.'

'"They stood side by side leaning on the rail, separated by less than the width of the woman's hair ribbon which fluttered in the wind. Together they said farewell to Venice as the palace of the Doges faded from view in a pale flush of red like a second sunset."'

'What is a Doge?'

'That isn't important. The Doges were the ancient rulers of Venice. I don't know for how many generations they ruled, but anyway their palace is still standing even to this day.'

'Who are the man and woman in the story?'

'I don't know either. That's what is so interesting. It doesn't matter what their previous relationship might have been. Don't you see that there is something interesting about that situation, which is independent of what comes before or after, just as there is about you and I being together here?'

'I suppose so. They seem to be on a boat.'

'It's immaterial whether they are on a boat or the top of a hill; just take it as it's written. And before you ask why, as I can see you're going to, I'll tell you. It's because if you probe for these details you turn yourself into a detective.'

'Ha, ha, ha, ha. In that case I won't ask.'

'The average novel invariably reads like a detective's report. It is drab and tedious because it is never objective.'

'Let's get on with the next instalment of objectivity. What happens after that?'

'"Venice sank lower and lower until it became scarcely more than a line stretching across the horizon. The line broke into a series of dashes as here and there a column rose up into the opal sky. Gradually these too disappeared from view, and were finally followed by the very highest belfry which had towered over all. It's gone, said the woman. Having left Venice she felt as free as the wind, but the knowledge that one day she would have to return gripped at her heart like a vice. The man and woman stared out at the darkening bay, watching the stars which were becoming more numerous every minute, and the gentle movement of the foam-flecked sea. As he held her hand, the man had the feeling that he had taken hold of a still quivering bow-string."'

'That doesn't sound very objective to me.'

'No, but you can listen to it objectively. Still, if you don't like it I'll skip a little, shall I?'

'No, I don't mind it.'

'Well, if you don't, I certainly don't.—Now let's see, where was I?—er—this part is rather complicated. It's very difficult to trans—I mean to read.'

'Leave it out if it's difficult.'

'All right, let's just pick out the best parts. "Just for tonight", says the woman. "Only one night? No, that's too cruel. We'll make it many, many nights."'

'Who says that, the man or the woman?'

'The man. If you remember, the woman doesn't want to go back to Venice, so the man says this to console her.—

"As he lay there on the deck in the small hours of the morning, his head pillowed on a coiled halyard, the memory of that moment when he had clasped the woman's hand—a moment like a single drop of hot blood—swept over him in a great wave. Staring up into the darkness he determined that come what may he would save her from falling into the abyss of a forced marriage. Having decided this he closed his eyes.—"'

'What happens to the woman?'

'"The woman wandered along the road in a daze, as though she had no clear idea of where she was going. Like one who has been spirited away through the air, only unfathomable mystery . . . ." It becomes rather difficult to read after that. Somehow it doesn't make a complete sentence— "only unfathomable mystery"—There doesn't seem to be a verb.'

'Who needs a verb? It's perfect as it is.'

'Hm?'

Suddenly there came a deep rumbling, followed by the creaking and groaning of every tree on the mountainside. As we turned instinctively towards each other, I noticed that the solitary camellia spray which was in a small vase on my desk was swinging to and fro. 'Earthquake!' gasped the woman in a frightened whisper, and relaxing her formal kneeling posture, she sank sideways into a sitting position and rested her arms on the desk. Slowly our two bodies moved closer together. At that moment with a staccato beating of wings a pheasant flew out of the nearby bamboo thicket.

'A pheasant,' I said looking out of the window.

'Where?' asked the woman relaxing still more and leaning her body against me. Our faces were now almost touching, and I could feel the breath coming from her delicate nostrils lightly brush against my moustache.

'Objectivity, remember?' she said firmly, and quickly sat upright again.

'Of course,' I replied promptly.

Outside, the spring rainwater which filled a hollow in one of the rocks had been goaded into drowsy motion by the earthquake. Since, however, the tremors which passed up through the rock had set the body of water moving as a whole, the surface remained unruffled save for a filigree pattern of lightly etched lines. The impression this gave was one of passive activity, so to speak. The reflection of wild cherry blossoms which had hitherto bathed in the pool undisturbed was now spreading and contracting, writhing and squirming in sympathy with the ripples. What struck me as extremely interesting, however, was that in spite of all its contortions it was still clearly recognisable as cherry blossom.

'That's delightful,' I said. 'It is pretty and it has variety. To be attractive motion must be just like that.'

'If only people could ride the blows of life in that fashion, they would be secure however much they were pushed around.'

'That would only be possible if they were detached and objective.'

'Ha, ha, ha, ha. You really do love objectivity, don't you?'

'You're not exactly averse to it yourself. That business of the wedding gown yesterday . . .' I began accusingly.

'Will you give me a nice present?' she asked suddenly in a coaxing voice.

'Why?'

'Well you said you wanted to see me in my bridal gown, so I put it on for you specially.'

'Who, I did?'

'I was told that a certain artist who had come across the

mountains was kind enough to make such a request to the old lady up at the tea-house.'

I could not think of any appropriate reply to this. The woman went on with scarcely a pause for breath.

'It's a waste of time to put oneself out to be obliging to someone as forgetful as you, isn't it?' she said, her voice filled with derision and bitterness. This was the second shaft in quick succession which she had released at point-blank range. The tide of battle was gradually turning against me, and I found it difficult to see how I was going to make up so much lost ground.

'And yesterday evening in the bathroom, that was also out of kindness then,' I said rallying slightly to meet the crisis.

There was no answer.

'I'm terribly sorry. How can I make it up to you?' I pressed on as much as I could, but with no effect. The woman just sat there with a far away expression on her face, staring at the scroll which had been written by the abbot Daitetsu. At length—

'Bamboo sweeps across the stairs,
But no dust rises
For 'tis but a shadow.'

She murmured the words softly to herself, and then turning to face me again she said, 'What did you say?' as though she had suddenly remembered that I had spoken. She asked the question in a deliberately loud voice, but I was not going to fall for that trick.

'I met the abbot earlier on,' I remarked demonstrating the same 'passive activity' as the pool of water which had been disturbed by the earthquake.

'The abbot of the Kankaiji temple? He's fat, isn't he?'

'He asked me to paint a Western style picture on a

fusuma. Those Zen priests do say the most ridiculous things, don't they?'

'That's probably why they get so fat.'

'I met a young man too.'

'I expect that was Kyuichi.'

'Yes, that's right.'

'You seem to know him very well.'

'No, I don't know anything about him except his name. He's a rather taciturn person, isn't he?'

'No, he's just shy. He's still only a boy.'

'A boy? He must be as old as you.'

'Ha, ha, ha, ha. Do you think so?—He's my cousin you know. He just came to say good-bye because he's off to the front.'

'Is he staying here?'

'No, he's at my elder brother's place.'

'Oh, so he came here especially to have tea?'

'He prefers plain warm water to tea. It would have been better if my father hadn't invited him, but he would do it. I expect Kyuichi was dreadfully bored. I would have let him go before it finished if I'd been at home, but . . . .'

'I heard from the abbot that you'd gone out somewhere. He wondered whether you were on one of your lone walks.'

'Yes, I was. I took a stroll down by the Kagami pond.'

'I'd like to go there too.'

'Yes, you must go and see it.'

'Is it a good place for painting?'

'It's a good place for dying.'

'I have no intention of dying yet a while.'

'I have. Perhaps very soon.'

I looked up sharply, thinking this too forthright a joke for a woman to make. I was surprised to find, however, that she was serious.

'Will you paint a beautiful picture of me floating in the

water?—Not in any pain you understand—but floating easily and peacefully in my eternal rest.'

'What!?'

'Aha! That startled you. Go on, admit it. That startled you, didn't it?'

The woman slid gracefully to her feet, and having walked the three paces to the door, paused on her way out to look back at me with a trace of a smile hovering about her lips. For a long time I just sat there gazing vacantly into space.

✦ 10 ✦

I went down to have a look at the Kagami pond. The path behind the Kankaiji temple dipped between cryptomeria trees into the valley beneath. Here it forked, and both branches skirted the perimeter of the pond before climbing the opposite hillside. The area around the pond was covered with a thick scrub of variegated bamboo. Indeed, in some places this grew up so densely on either hand that it became almost impossible to proceed quietly. The water was visible between the trees, but never having been there before, I had no idea how far it extended in either direction. I walked on, and presently was able to see that the pond was smaller than I had imagined, being less than a quarter of a mile in length. It was extraordinarily irregular in outline, and here and there down by the water's edge there were many natural boulders. The constant outcrops which thrust forward into the waves formed an unsymmetrical contour which could scarcely be called pond-shaped.

The valley was filled with hundreds of trees of many different kinds, some of which had not as yet put forth their spring buds. In some places, where the branches were sparse enough to allow the spring sunshine to stream through in undiminished glory, there were even plants and flowers sprouting up beneath the trees. Among these I caught an occasional glimpse of the pale form of a miniature violet. In Japan, violets always give the impression that they are dozing. By no stretch of the imagination could one call them 'a flash of divine inspiration' as did one Western poet. It was just as my thoughts reached this point that I realized I had stopped walking. I decided to remain where I was until I grew bored with the place, and considered myself very lucky to be able to do so. If I had done such a thing in Tokyo I would either have been run down immediately by a tram, or moved on by a policeman. In the city they are unable to tell the difference between a law-abiding citizen and a vagrant. Moreover, they pay enormous salaries to detectives who are the biggest rogues of all.

I eased my law-abiding buttocks down on to the cushioning grass. One could remain in such a place as this for five or six days without the fear of anybody making a complaint. That is the beauty of Nature. It is true that if forced Nature can act ruthlessly and without remorse, but on the other hand she is free of all perfidy, since her attitude is the same towards everyone who harasses her. There are any amount of people with the ability to judge without fear or favour between Iwasaki and Mitsui,[1] but only Nature could, with icy indifference, set at nought the might of all the princes since time began. Her virtue is far beyond the corrupting reach of this world, and she looks down with an absolute impartiality from the seat of judgment which she has established in infinity. It is a much wiser policy to plant acre after acre of orchids and lead one's life in solitude encompassed by their sheltering stems, than to surround oneself with the hoi-polloi and so court the same pointless misanthropic disgust as befell Timon of Athens. Society is forever holding forth about fairness and justice. If it really believes these to be of such importance, it might do well

[1] Iwasaki and Mitsui were the founders of the Mitsubishi and Mitsui companies respectively. These were and still are two of the largest concerns in Japan.

to kill off a few dozen petty criminals per day, and use their carcasses to fertilize and give life to countless fields of flowers.

I felt somehow that my thoughts had become too serious. After all, I had not come down to the Kagami pond merely to make adolescent observations on life. I took out a cigarette from the packet of *Shikishima* in my sleeve, and struck a match. I felt the match-head rasp against the box, but I could see no flame. Nevertheless I held the match to the end of my cigarette and inhaled. It was not until I finally saw the smoke coming out of my nostrils, however, that I became aware that the cigarette really was alight. A tiny wisp of smoke rising from the matchstick in the short grass, formed a long-tailed dragon which went rapidly to join its ancestors in eternity. I slithered slowly down to the water's edge. The grassy bank which had served me as a cushion ran right on into the natural pond, but I managed to stop just in time to save my feet from a tepid soaking. Having come to a halt, I squatted there staring into the water.

The part of the pond near where I was sitting was not very deep, and on the bottom I could see long slender tendrils of weed which looked as though they had given up the ghost. This is the only phrase I can think of which describes their appearance. The pampas grass up on the hill knew how to attract and yield to the touch of the wind, but this weed was waiting for some sign of affection from a flirtatious wave. Lying submerged in water which was obviously not going to move in a hundred years, it had preened itself and struck a pose waiting for the time when it too could play the coquette. It had waited in vain through an endless succession of days and nights, its long unsatiated desire to love expressed in the tip of every stem, until now it led a paralysed existence, unable to die.

Picking two handy stones out of the grass, I stood up. Out of kindness I threw one of the stones at the patch of water directly in front of me. As I did so two bubbles came gurgling to the surface, but disappeared immediately. Those two words, 'disappeared immediately', kept echoing around in my brain. Peering down into the water, I saw that about three strands of weed had begun to move sleepily, and I was just about to cry out, 'You've been noticed,' when a muddy cloud rose up from the bottom and hid them from view. 'May your soul rest in peace.'

I flung the next stone resolutely out into the centre of the pond where it made a dull 'plop'. The imperturbable water, however, took not the slightest notice. I had now grown tired of throwing stones, and leaving my colour-box and hat where they were, I walked off a few yards to the right up a gentle incline.

I was now standing beneath the spreading branches of a large tree, and suddenly felt cold. Over on the far bank camellia bushes bloomed among the shadows. Camellia leaves are too deep a green, and have no air of light-heartedness even when seen in bright sunlight. These particular bushes were in a silent huddle, set back five or six yards in an angle between the rocks, and had it not been for the blossoms I should not have known that there was anything there at all. Those blossoms! I could not of course have counted them all if I had spent the whole day at it; yet somehow their brilliance made me want to try. The trouble with camellia blossoms is that although they are brilliant they are in no way cheerful. You find that in spite of yourself your attention is attracted by the violent blaze of colour, but once you look at them they give you an uncanny feeling. They are the most deceitful of all flowers. Whenever I see a wild camellia growing in the heart of the mountains, I am reminded of a beautiful enchantress who lures men on with her dark eyes, and then in a flash injects her smiling venom into their veins. By the time they realise that they have been tricked it is too late. No sooner had I caught sight of the camellias opposite than I wished I

135

had not done so. Theirs was no ordinary red. It was a colour of eye-searing intensity, which contained some indefinable quality. Pear blossoms drooping despondently in the rain only arouse in me a feeling of pity, and the cool aronia bathed in pale moonlight strikes the chords of love. The quality of camellia blossoms, however, is altogether different. It speaks of darkness and evil, and is something to be feared. It is, moreover apparent in every gaudy petal. These blossoms do not give the impression that they are flattering you, nor do they show that they are deliberately trying to entice you. They will live in perfect serenity for hundreds of years far from the eyes of man in the shadow of the mountains, flaring into bloom and falling to earth with equal suddenness. But let a man glance at them even for an instant, and for him it is the end. He will never be able to break free from the spell of the enchantress. No, theirs is no ordinary red. It is the red of an executed criminal's blood which automatically attracts men's gaze and fills their hearts with sorrow.

As I stood watching, a red flower hit the water, providing the only movement in the stillness of spring. After a while it was followed by another. Camellia flowers never drift down petal by petal, but drop from the branch intact. Although this in itself is not particularity unpleasant since it merely suggests an indifference to parting, the way in which they remain whole even when they have landed is both gross and offensive to the eye. If they continue like this, I thought, they will stain the whole pond red. Already the water in the immediate vicinity of the peacefully floating blossoms seemed to have a reddish tint. Yet another flower dropped and remained as motionless as if it had come to rest on the bank. There goes another. I wondered whether this one would sink. Perhaps over the years millions of camellia blossoms would steep in the water and, having surrendered their colour, would rot and eventually turn to mud on the bottom. If that should happen, then they might imperceptibly build up the bed of this old stagnating pond until in thousands of years time the whole area would return to the plain it had been originally. Now a large bloom plunged downwards like a blood-smeared phantom. Another fell, and another, striking the water like a shower of pattering raindrops.

Wondering how it would be to paint a beautiful woman floating in such a pond as this, I walked back down to the water's edge. Here I smoked another cigarette, and fell to musing once more. Suddenly the words which O-Nami at the hotel had said to me jokingly came flooding back into my mind, and I felt as though my heart were a raft that was being pitched and tossed by great waves. Suppose I painted *her* floating in the water beneath those camellias, with blossom after blossom dropping on her from above. I wanted to create the impression that the camellia blossoms would continue to fall, and the woman remain floating there throughout all eternity, but I was not sure that this would make a good picture. According to *Laokoon*—but who cares about that? Providing that a painting expresses the desired feeling, it makes not the slightest difference whether or not it conforms to any principles. I knew, however, that it was going to be no easy task to express so non-human a concept as eternity while using a human subject. First and foremost was the problem of the girl's face. I wanted to use O-Nami's face, but her expressions were all wrong. Her look of suffering would be so overpowering that it would destroy the whole effect, while her outbursts of immoderate gaiety would be even worse. Thinking that perhaps I ought to use someone else's face, I ran through all the women I knew counting them off on my fingers, but none of them was satisfactory. O-Nami was the most suitable after all, yet there was something lacking. That much I realised, but since I could not put my finger on the deficiency, it was impossible to make the appropriate alteration to her expression as I pictured it in my mind. If I added jealousy, the feeling of uneasiness would be too strong. What about hatred? No, that was too violent. Anger? No, that would completely shatter the harmony. I dismissed bitterness because, with the exception of the poetic bitterness of love, I consider it too vulgar. Having thought over various other possibilities, the answer suddenly dawned on me. I had forgotten that there exists among the many emotions one called compassion. It is unknown to the gods, and yet it is the very emotion that can elevate man to near-deity. There was not a trace of compassion in O-Nami's expression; that was what was missing. The instant I saw a flicker of this emotion pass across her features roused by some momentary impulse, I would be able to complete my picture; but when or even if that time would come I had no way of knowing. Her usual expression was only a faint mocking smile accompanied by a frown which showed a burning determination to win at all costs. This by itself was useless to me.

I heard the harsh rustling sound of someone treading among the bamboo undergrowth, and the plan of my picture, which was two thirds completed in my head, crumbled. Looking up I saw a man going towards the Kankaiji temple, having presumably come down the neighbouring hillside. He was wearing a tight-sleeved kimono, and carried a bundle of faggots on his back.

'Lovely weather,' he said, untying a towel from around his head. As he bowed the blade of a hatchet thrust into his belt flashed in the sunlight. He was a powerfully built man of about forty, and I had a feeling that I had seen him somewhere before. He treated me with the easy familiarity of an old friend.

'Do you paint too, sir?' he asked noticing my open colour-box.

'Yes. I came down to have a look at this pond because I thought I might paint it, but this is a lonely place, isn't it? Nobody seems to come here.'

'Yes, it certainly is isolated. . . . You must have had a terrible time of it in all that rain up in the pass.'

'Eh? Oh, you're the packhorse driver I met there.'

'That's right. I cut firewood like this, and take it down to the town,' said Gembei, for it was he. Lowering his bundle to the ground, he sat down on it and took out a tobacco pouch. This was so old that it was impossible to tell whether it was paper or leather. I offered him a match.

'Don't you find it a job having to cross the mountains every day like that?'

'No, I'm used to it. Besides, I only go once every three days, or sometimes every four days; it all depends.'

'I wouldn't want to do it even once in four days.'

'Ha, ha, ha, ha. I try and keep it down to once in four days because the trip's hard on the horse.'

'So the horse is more important than you, is he? Ha, ha, ha, ha.'

'Well, I wouldn't quite say that . . . .'

'By the way, this pond is extremely old, isn't it? How long has it been here, for heaven's sake?'

'For ages.'

'For ages? What do you mean by ages?'

'Well, from a very long time ago.'

'A very long time ago. I see.'

'I know it's been here for years and years, because this is where the Shioda girl drowned herself.'

'Shioda? At the hot spring, you mean?'

'That's right.'

'You say she drowned herself? But she's still alive and well.'

'No, no, no. I'm not talking about the present Mr. Shioda's daughter. This was years ago.'

'Years ago? How long?'

'Oh, way back in olden times.'

'And why did *she* drown herself?'

'It seems, sir, that she was just as beautiful as this Mr. Shioda's daughter.'

'Go on.'

'One day a bōronji came along . . .'

'You mean one of those wandering minstrels?'

'Yes. You know, they used to go from place to place playing a flute, and begging. Well, Shioda's beautiful daughter saw him while he was staying at their place, and it was a case of love at first sight.—What they call Fate, I believe. Anyhow, she said she simply had to marry him, and burst into tears.'

'Did she? Well, well, well.'

'But her father wouldn't hear of it. He said that a bōronji wasn't a fit husband for her, and quickly threw him out of the house. The girl followed him, and then when she got as far as this she threw herself into the water from somewhere near that pine tree you can see over there.—It caused a tremendous stir in the village.—The girl had a mirror with her when she drowned herself, so the story goes. That's why even to this day this is called the Kagami pond.'

'I see. So this pond has already been somebody's grave, has it?'

'Yes, a very extraordinary affair, indeed.'

'How many years ago was this supposed to have happened?'

'Oh, years and years back.—But you know sir, between you and me . . .'

'Yes?'

'There's been somebody mad in every generation of the Shioda family.'

'You don't say.'

'There's a curse on them, and no mistake. Everybody

140

makes fun of O-Nami Shioda because they say she's become strange lately.'

'Ha, ha, ha, ha. Nonsense.'

'Maybe you're right. But her old lady was definitely queer in the head.'

'Does she live with the family?'

'No, she died last year.'

'Hm,' was all the reply I made as I watched a thin coil of smoke rise from the tobacco ash which my companion had knocked from his pipe. Gembei shouldered his load again and left.

I had come to this pond to paint, but it was clear that if I continued musing and listening to such tales I would not produce a solitary picture even if I remained here for days. Since I had gone to the trouble of bringing my colour-box with me, I felt that the least I could do today would be to make some preliminary sketches of the place. Fortunately the scenery opposite would need very little rearranging to turn it into a picture, and I thought that I might make some sort of attempt at painting it.

In an angle of the tortuous shore-line, away to the right, a rock lifted its rugged bulk over ten feet out of the thick stagnant water. The bamboo which I mentioned before completely covered the precipitous side of the rock and reached right down to the water's edge. At the top, an enormous ivy-mantled pine tree about three arm spans in circumference had wrenched itself askew and leaned more than half its length out over the water. It was probably from the top of that rock that the woman had jumped clutching the mirror to her breast.

I sat down on my tripod and cast an appraising eye over the materials that would go to make up the picture. There was the pine tree, the bamboo, the rock and the water. I could not decide, however, how much of the latter I ought to include, for the ten foot high rock cast a reflection of equal length into the depths and the bamboo was so clearly mirrored that it appeared to have continued its luxuriant growth right out into the water. Moreover, the image of the enormous towering pine tree stretched far across the pond. It was obvious that I would not get the whole scene on to the canvas in the proportions in which they appeared to me, and this led me to think that it might be interesting to paint just the reflections. I felt sure that I would astonish people if I showed them a canvas which depicted only water and reflections, and claimed that it was a picture. Mere astonishment, however, was worthless. I wanted to find some way to present these things which would astonish people because it forced them to admit that they did constitute a picture. Staring intently at the surface of the water, I sought for a solution.

Strangely enough I could think of no expedient while looking at just the reflections, and I felt that I needed to compare them with their actual counterparts. I allowed my gaze to travel slowly from the tip of the rock's reflection up to where image joined reality, and then on again upwards appreciating as I did so not only the overall atmosphere of permanence and solidity, but also every detail of the wrinkled surface. When finally my eyes reached the top of that dangerous rock, I dropped my sketchbook and brush in surprise, and froze like a toad beneath the hypnotic stare of a snake.

The shadows of the spring evening were beginning to deepen, and the last rays of sunlight slanted down through the green foliage making a patchwork quilt of light and shade as a backdrop to the rock. Into this I could see a face clearly interwoven. It was the face of the woman who had startled me as she stood beneath the aronia blossoms; who had startled me by entering my room as a phantom; who had startled me when wearing her wedding gown; and who had startled me in the bathroom.

For a second I sat rooted to the spot with my gaze fixed on the woman's face. She too stood perfectly immobile on top of the rock, drawing her supple body up to its full height. It was an exquisite moment.

Suddenly without thinking I leaped to my feet, and as I did so she swung round nimbly. I had scarcely time to glimpse a snatch of red like a camellia blossom in her obi before she jumped down the other side and was gone. The evening sun rested gently on the tree tops, subtly dyeing the trunk of the great pine, and making the bamboo look an even darker green.

Once again I had been startled.

✦ 11 ✦

Thinking it a pity to waste the spring twilight by staying indoors, I had come out for a walk. Going up the flight of stone steps which led to the Kankaiji temple I had made up the following lines to express the simple child-like awe with which the sight of the stars filled me.

> Turn your face up—two, three,
> And count—four, five,
> The stars in the spring sky—six, seven, eight . . . .

There was no particular business that I had wanted to discuss with the abbot, nor had I even felt the desire for a chat. I had simply left the hotel on the spur of the moment and strolled along aimlessly until I came to the large stone lantern set at the foot of the steps. For a while I had just stood there running my hand lightly over the stone surface on which was carved, 'No alcohol or strongly flavoured vegetables are to be brought into the temple.' Then quite suddenly I had felt a surge of happiness and had begun to climb.

In *Tristram Shandy*, Sterne states that there is no method of writing more in accordance with the will of God than his. He says that he composes the opening gambit by his own efforts, but that thereafter it is a matter of fervent prayer and leaving the movement of the pen to God. Accordingly he has, of course, no idea of what he is going to write or of his ultimate destination. He only holds the pen, and it is God who does the writing. Thus, apparently, he is free from all responsibility. My stroll, and Sterne's method of writing had much in common, since they both drank at the well of irresponsibility. On my side, however, the lack of responsibility was greater, for I had not even relied on God. Sterne got rid of his responsibility by thrusting it on to his Heavenly Father, but I, who have no God to take it from me, finally dispose of mine by throwing it into a ditch with the rest of the rubbish.

I had no intention of climbing the stone steps if the ascent should prove laborious. At the first signs of fatigue I would have withdrawn from the fray. However, stopping on the first step, I had unaccountably felt a sense of pleasure, and so had proceeded to the second. On the second step I had had the urge to compose a poem. In silence I regarded my shadow. There had seemed something strange and mysterious about the way in which it was arrested and broken by the edge of the third step; and because of this air of mystery, I had continued my climb. I had gazed up at the heavens and seen a host of small stars blinking out at me from the sleepy depths. This had struck me as poetic, and once again I had gone on, until in this way I had eventually reached the top.

Here I had been reminded of something that happened a long time ago when I went on a trip to Kamakura. I had been roaming around having a look at the five most famous temples there, and I am almost certain that this particular incident took place at an outer shrine of the Enkakuji temple. I was slowly plodding up a flight of stone steps, just as at the Kankaiji, when a priest wearing a saffron robe and with a flat-crowned head emerged from the gateway at the top. I was going up, and the priest was coming down. When we drew level he asked me sharply where I was going. I stopped and replied that I wanted to have a look round the temple grounds. 'There's nothing to see,' he said curtly, and hurried away down the steps. His unexpectedly frank and easy manner took me unawares, and I was still standing at the top of the steps watching his flat-crowned head bob from side to side, when he disappeared from view among some cryptomeria trees. During the entire descent he had not given a single backward glance. Zen priests certainly are interesting people, I thought. They are always short, sharp and to the point. I trudged in through the temple gate and looked about. There was not a living soul in either the priests' quarters or in the main hall. The whole place looked desolate. On seeing this I felt elated. The thought that there were in the world people as straightforward as the priest I had just met who dealt with you frankly somehow reassured me. It was not that I was well versed in Zen Buddhism, for to tell the truth I did not know the first thing about it. No, it was just that I was taken with the attitude of the priest with the singularly shaped head.

The world is full of the most terrible people who are importunate, coarse, niggling and, to crown it all, brazen. Indeed, it is incomprehensible why some of them ever showed their faces on earth in the first place. They assume airs and graces, but in reality there is nothing great about them at all. Because of their expansive appearance, the fickle world frequently casts its spotlight on them, and they labour under the misapprenhension that this is fame. They will set a detective on your tail for five or ten years to reckon up how many times you break wind, and they think this is Life. Moreover, they will, on occasion, leap out in front of you and impart such unsolicited information as, 'You farted x number of times'. When they tell you this face to face, you may listen and make a note of it for future reference. But the refrain, 'You farted x number of time', often comes from behind. If you say they are a nuisance, they do it all the more. If you tell them to stop it, they redouble their efforts. Even if you say that you know, they will still repeat, 'You farted x number of times'. This is their idea of how to live with their fellow creatures. They are, of course, free to formulate their own principles for living, providing that these do not include telling people, 'You farted, you farted'. It is only common decency to desist from any course of action which is going to inconvenience others. If, however, they cannot find such a course of action, then I shall have no choice but to adopt farting as my policy; and if that should ever happen, it will be a sorry day for Japan.

My aimless wandering on that beautiful spring evening at the Kankaiji temple was a practical manifestation of refinement. If inspiration came to me, I would accept its coming as the reason for my walk; if it left me, then its departure would become my reason. If I should compose a poem, to compose would have been my object; if I should not, then my aim would have been not to compose. Moreover, I was not inflicting myself on anybody. Thus mine was an unimpeachable principle. Counting how many times others break wind is a policy of personal attack to which farting itself is a legitimate means of defence. I, however, in climbing the steps of the temple as I had just done, was pursuing a policy of 'live and let live, and follow wherever Fate may lead.'

Turn your face up—two, three,
And count—four, five,
The stars in the spring sky—six, seven, eight . . .

By the time I had made up these lines I was above the field of light shed by the stone lantern, and thus was able to discern through the dusk the softly shimmering surface of the vernal sea which lay unrolled beneath me like a broad patterned sash. I now passed through the gateway. I was no longer in the mood for composing Chinese style quatrains, and so decided upon a policy of stopping immediately.

On the right of the stone-paved path which led to the priests' living quarters was a wild azalea hedge, beyond which, I imagined, would be the burial ground. To the left stood the main temple hall. It was a tall imposing building whose tiled roof had taken on a dull sheen in the moonlight. Looking up I became sensible of an air of great antiquity: of untold moons who had poured their light on innumerable tiles. Somewhere I could hear the repeated cooing of pigeons. They seemed to be living beneath the ridge of the roof. I did not know whether it was my imagination, but I fancied that the eaves were flecked with white. Pigeon droppings, perhaps.

Beneath the overhang of the eaves I could see a line of weird shadowy forms. They did not look like trees, and yet they were obviously too tall to be flowers or clumps of grass. The impression they gave was that the 'Praying Spirits' painted by Iwasa Matabei[1] had ceased praying and begun dancing. They danced in a well-ordered row which extended from one end of the main hall to the other, accompanied by the equally well-ordered line of their own shadows. They had probably found the beauty of the evening irresistible, and paused only long enough to persuade each other before abandoning their gongs, bell-hammers[2] and records of sacred offerings, and coming here to dance.

When I drew closer, the forms proved to be great cactus plants about seven or eight feet tall. Their green gourds, which were the size of sponge cucumbers, resembled in shape large flattened soup spoons with the handles pointing downwards. The plants were, in fact, composed of a series of these gourds each sprouting from the stem of the one

[1] Iwasa Matabei, Japanese artist (1578-1650)
[2] Used in Buddhist services.

beneath, and stretching up and up in a spatulate progression which would eventually end Heaven only knew where. It seemed likely that these cacti would, this very evening, break their way through the eaves and emerge on to the roof above. Undoubtedly, the 'spoons' suddenly materialized out of thin air fully grown, for I could not imagine the older ones giving birth to young which gradually grew to maturity in the fullness of time. This persistent sticking of one 'spoon' upon another was somehow eccentric. There can be few plants as comical as the cactus, and yet it affects an air of composed indifference. A certain Zen priest when asked by a pupil, 'What is Buddha?' is said to have replied, 'That oak tree in the garden.' If, however, I were asked the same question, I should answer without a moment's hesitation, 'That lord of all plants: a cactus in the moonlight.'

When I was a boy, I read an account by the classical Chinese writer Ch'ao Pu-chih of a journey he once made, and there is one passage which I can still quote from memory. I repeated the words over to myself.

It was the ninth month of the year. Not a cloud obscured the vault of heaven. The dew lay pure upon the ground and the mountains were deserted. The moon was bright, and the stars, which shone brilliantly, seemed to have been casually scattered across the sky. Cast on the shōji were the shadows of a thousand bamboo stems from which the passing wind drew a ceaseless rustling whisper. Between the bamboos could be seen a host of plum and palm trees like hobgoblins with hair in spiky disarray. My companions discussed this with each other, and it so disturbed them that they were unable to sleep. The next morning we departed.

Suddenly I burst out laughing. Given the right combination of time and place I too might have been disturbed by these cactus plants, and gone scuttling down the mountainside as soon as I had caught sight of them. I touched the spines and felt them prick my fingers.

Having followed the stone path to the end, I bore to the left and came to the misericord in front of which stood a large magnolia. I should say that this tree had a girth of almost an arm-span, and in height too it was considerable, being taller than the building. Above my head was tier upon tier of branches, and finally, perched on top of all, the moon. Usually when a tree has so many branches you can see very little of the sky from below, and if there are blossoms as well, then it is completely blotted out. The magnolia, however, is not cluttered with scores of useless twigs which throw the eyes of the person beneath into confusion. Thus, however many branches there may be, the patches of sky between them are always sharply defined. Even the blossoms themselves are distinct, and from far below one may still make out each individual bloom. It is impossible to judge the extent of this swarm of blossoms, yet nevertheless each one is a separate entity, and between them the pale blue of the sky is clearly visible. Magnolia blossoms are not of course pure white in colour, for stark unrelieved whiteness is too cold, and seems to be no more than a deliberately immodest device to attract men's eyes. No, they are different. They purposely avoid extreme whiteness, and their warm creamy tint is an expression of gentility and self-depreciation. Standing on the flagstones gazing upward, I was lost, for a while, in contemplation of how this pagoda of modest blossoms seemed to rise and spread endlessly into the vastness of space. My whole attention was held by the flowers. For me not a single leaf existed. The following lines formed in my mind.

Above, the sometime realm of star and moon
Is all magnolia to my enraptured gaze.

Somewhere the pigeons were still cooing softly to each other.

I entered the porch of the misericord. The verandah which ran along the side of the building was completely open, seemingly indicating that this was a world where thieves were unknown. There were of course no dogs to bark.

The only response to the call of 'Excuse me,' with which I announced my visit was a deathly hush. Once again I called out in the hope that someone would come and show me the way. 'Is anybody there?' All I heard was the 'coo, coo, coo' of the pigeons.

'Is anybody there?' This time I shouted the words. An answering bellow sounded far off within the building. In all the times I had visited people's houses I had never received such a reply as this. At length there came the sound of footsteps approaching the verandah, and the light from a taper fell on the other side of the shōji. Suddenly a young priest was standing before me. It was Ryonen.

'Is the abbot at home?'

'Yes, he is. May I ask what you want him for?'

'Will you tell him, please, that the artist who is staying at the hot spring is here?'

'Oh, you're the artist? Come on in.'

'Hadn't you better tell the abbot I'm here first?'

'No, that's all right.'

I slipped off my wooden clogs and stepped up on to the verandah.

'You're a rather ill-mannered artist, aren't you?'

'Why?'

'Put your clogs straight. Look here,' he said thrusting the taper almost under my nose. In the middle of one of the black posts of the porchway, no more than five feet from the ground was a small piece of paper on which I could just make out some writing.

'Read that. It says, "First, set thine own house in order."'

'I see,' I replied, carefully arranging my clogs.

We walked along the verandah, followed its right-angled turn, and came to the abbot's room which was next to the main hall. Ryonen knelt respectfully and eased open the shōji.

'Er, I'm sorry to trouble you sir, but the artist from Shioda's is here.' His extremely apologetic attitude struck me as rather amusing.

'Is he? Show him in.'

Ryonen withdrew, and I went in. The room was very small. On the hearth which had been cut in the centre, an iron kettle was singing. The abbot, who was sitting across the room, had been reading.

'Come, in, come in,' he said removing his spectacles and pushing his book to one side. 'Ryonen! Ryo—ne—n!'

'Ye—es?'

'Bring a cushion for our guest, will you?'

'Ye—es,' came Ryonen's protracted reply from some way off.

'It's nice to see you. I expect you got terribly bored.'

'There was such a beautiful moon that I thought I'd take a stroll.'

'It is beautiful,' he agreed opening the shōji.

Just across the level garden, whose only contents were two stepping stones and a pine tree, was the edge of the cliff, and there spread out immediately beneath me in the evening was the sea. Here and there on the water was the flicker of fishing-fires. Those in the farthest distance had forsaken the sea for the sky, presumably with the intention of becoming stars.

'What a wonderful view, Abbot. Don't you think it's a pity to keep the shōji shut?'

'It is, of course, but I see it every evening.'

'But you could never tire of scenery like this, however

many evenings you saw it. I'd go without sleep to look at it.'

'Ha, ha, ha, ha. Obviously, because you're an artist. But you and I are a little different.'

'But, Abbot, if you can appreciate the beauty of it, then you too are an artist.'

'Yes, I suppose that's true, though I've never got farther than drawing pictures of Dharma Buddha. Speaking of Dharma, there's a picture of him here. My predecessor painted it. I think it's very well done.'

Sure enough there was a scroll painting of Dharma Buddha hanging in a small alcove. As a picture it was, however, atrocious. All that could be said for it was that it was not vulgar or worldly, and the artist had made no attempt to cover up his lack of skill. It was an unsophisticated painting.

'It's an unsophisticated piece of work, isn't it?'

'That's quite sufficient for a priest. Providing that it expresses his mood . . .'

'Well, it's better than being skilfully executed but vulgar.'

'Ha, ha, ha, ha. I accept the compliment. By the way, have they instituted a Doctor of Painting degree recently?'

'No, there's no such thing as a Doctor of Painting.'

'Oh, isn't there? Anyway, I met one the other day.'

'You did?'

'I suppose to get a doctorate you have to be a remarkable person.'

'Yes, I suppose you do.'

'You know, it seems to me that there ought to be a doctorate for painting. I wonder why there isn't one.'

'If you take that view, there ought to be a doctorate for priests too, oughtn't there?'

'Ha, ha, ha, ha, ha. Perhaps that's so.—Now what was his name, that fellow I met recently? I ought to have his card here somewhere.'

'Where did you meet him, in Tokyo?'

'No, here. I haven't been up to Tokyo in twenty years. I hear that recently they've started running those tramcar things. I'd rather like to have a ride on one.'

'You wouldn't like it at all. They're too noisy.'

'Maybe you're right. They say that those of little learning disbelieve and ridicule the greatest achievements, and those of little experience fear all things. If that's the case, perhaps an old yokel like me, far from enjoying a tram ride, would be upset by it.'

'It wouldn't upset you. You just wouldn't find it interesting, that's all.'

'Perhaps you're right.'

Steam was now issuing steadily from the spout of the kettle. The abbot took out the tea things from a small chest of drawers, and poured me a cup of tea.

'Have some tea. It's very poor quality, I'm afraid. Not nearly as good as old Mr. Shioda's.'

'I'm sure it's very nice.'

'You seem to do quite a lot of wandering about from place to place. This is so that you can paint, is it?'

'Yes. All I take with me is my colour-box, but whether I actually produce a picture or not doesn't worry me.'

'So these trips are half for pleasure, are they?'

'Yes, I suppose you could say that. The fact is, I don't like having people count how many times I break wind.'

Zen priest though he was, this was one metaphor that apparently the abbot could not understand.

'What do you mean by "counting how many times you break wind"?'

'If you live in Tokyo for any length of time, you have your farts reckoned up.'

'How do you mean?'

'If that were all it wouldn't be so bad, but they do such unwarranted things as examining your backside to see whether your anus is triangular or square.'

'Ah, you mean the sanitary inspectors, I suppose.'

'No, I do not mean the sanitary inspectors. I mean detectives.'

'Detectives? Oh, I see, the police. What in the world is the use of the police? Are they really necessary, I wonder?'

'Well, artists certainly don't need them.'

'Nor do I. I have never yet had occasion to ask for their assistance.'

'No, I don't suppose you have.'

'But I don't see that it should bother you, however much they may count the times you break wind. Why don't you just ignore them? For all that they are police, they can do nothing unless you have committed some crime.'

'Even their fart-counting is insufferable.'

'I remember that my predecessor often used to tell me when I was a young priest, that a man cannot be said to have completed his education until he can stand at Nihonbashi in the centre of Tokyo, and lay bare his soul to the world without embarrassment. You too should strive towards that end, for if you attained it, you wouldn't have to take these trips to find peace of mind.'

'I could reach that state if I became a true artist.'

'Then you had better become one.'

'I can't all the time I'm having my farts counted.'

'Now look at O-Nami Shioda down where you're staying. She had so much weighing on her mind when she came back to her father's place after her divorce, that she could not bear it; and because she could not bear it she eventually came to me and asked for religious instruction. Recently she has improved tremendously. Look at her, she's now a highly rational woman.'

'Yes, I thought somehow that she was no ordinary woman.'

'She isn't. She has an extremely quick and lively mind.— Because of her, a young priest named Taian, who was here to finish his training, came to realise that destiny had ordained that he must devote himself to studying things of magnitude and not waste his time on trifling matters.—I believe he will now become a very wise man.'

The shadow of the pine tree fell across the garden. Far below, the sea, as though torn with indecision, sent back dim intermittent flashes to answer those in the sky.

'Look at the shadow of that pine tree,' I said.

'It's pretty, isn't it?'

'Just "pretty"?'

'Yes.'

'Not only is it pretty, it has the advantage of having nothing to fear even if the wind should blow.'

I drank the last drops of coarse tea, and then placing the cup upside down on the saucer, I stood up.

'I'll see you as far as the gate. Ryo—ne—n! Our guest is leaving.'

Accompanied by the abbot and Ryonen, I left the misericord. The pigeons were still cooing.

'There is nothing more charming than a pigeon. When I clap my hands, they fly to me. Shall I call them?'

The moon had grown brighter. In perfect silence the magnolia offered up its innumerable clouds of blossoms to the sky. There in the lonely emptiness of a spring night, the abbot clapped his hands sharply. The sound, however, died in the wind, and not a single pigeon came.

'They aren't going to come down. I thought they would.'

Ryonen looked at my face and smiled slightly. The abbot seemed to think that the pigeons would be able to see in the dark. He was an optimist.

At the gateway, I parted from my two companions. Looking back I could see two round shadows, one large and one small, on the paving. They changed places and disappeared in the direction of the misericord.

✦ 12 ✦

As I remember, it was Oscar Wilde who said that Christ possessed a superlatively artistic temperament. I do not know about Christ, but the abbot of the Kankaiji temple certainly qualifies for such a description. This is not to say that he was a man of good taste, or that he was conversant with all that was going on in the world about him. The scroll painting of Dharma Buddha that he had hung on the wall was one to which you would scarcely deign to apply the word picture, yet he felt that it was well done. He was convinced that there was such a degree as Doctor of Painting, and thought that pigeons could see in the dark. In spite of this, I still say that he can be termed an artist. His mind may be compared to the stomach, which being open at both ends allows nothing to accumulate. Since everything within his mind was constantly on the move and passed through freely, there was no sign that any deposit had remained behind to putrefy. Given just an added dash of discrimination, he would have been a perfect artist, at one with his surroundings wherever he might find himself, even in the course of the trivial round of everyday life. I, on the other hand, am the sort of person who can never become a true artist as long as he is having his farts counted by detectives. I can stand before an easel, and I can hold a palette, but that does not make an artist. Only in a place like this mountain village, even the name of which I do not

know, with my five foot odd of slender body totally sub-
merged in the darkening colours of spring, am I able to
achieve a truly artistic frame of mind. Once I have entered
this realm, all the beauty of the universe is mine, and without
painting even one square inch of canvas, indeed without so
much as lifting my brush, I become a great artist. I may not
equal Michelangelo in technique, nor be able to match
Raphael in skill, but in intrinsic artistic character I acknowl-
edge not the slightest inferiority to any artist, however great,
who has ever lived. Since I had come to the hot spring I had
not yet painted a single picture. This gives the impression that
I had only brought my colour-box with me to satisfy an idle
whim, and there may be those who will laugh and wonder
whether I thought I should become an artist merely by so
doing. For all their laughter, however, the fact remains that
here, I was a true artist, a fine artist. It does not follow that
everyone who achieves this state of mind that I was now in
will necessarily produce a masterpiece, but what can be said
is that it is impossible to produce a masterpiece unless you
do achieve this state of mind.

These, then, were my sentiments as I sat lingering over a
cigarette after breakfast. The sun had risen high above the
morning haze, and when I opened the shōji I could see green-
clad trees on a hill away to the rear of the house. There was
something remarkably diaphanous about them and they
looked unusually bright and fresh.

I have always thought the relationship between air, objects
and colours to be one of the most fascinating studies
that this world has to offer. The problem is whether one
should make the colours of prime importance and thus
bring out the quality of the air, or whether to disregard the
air in favour of stressing the objects themselves. There is
a third alternative, namely to make the air the most impor-
tant factor, and weave both colours and objects into it.

Every slight nuance in treatment produces a picture of a different mood, and this mood varies according to the individual tastes of the artist. This of course is an obvious point. Moreover, it is equally obvious that the mood is also automatically dictated by time and place. There is not a solitary bright landscape painted by an English artist. Perhaps the reason is that they dislike bright paintings, but with the air they have in England they could not paint one even if they wanted to. Goodall was an Englishman, but the quality of his colours is altogether different, as well it might be, for although English, he never once painted an English scene. He never chose a theme from his own country, but instead painted landscapes of Egypt and Persia where the air is infinitely clearer. His pictures are so vivid that everyone seeing them for the first time is astonished, and wonders how an Englishman was able to produce such clarity of colour.

Nothing can be done about the divergence of individual tastes, but we must at least bring out that quality of air and colour which is peculiar to Japan when we take a piece of Japanese scenery as our subject. You cannot say, 'This is a Japanese landscape,' of a picture in which the artist has slavishly copied colour tones as they appear in French paintings, however much you admire French art. You must meet Nature face to face, studying her every shape and form from dawn to dusk, until such time as you feel that you have found just the right colours. You must then grab your tripod and immediately rush out to record them on canvas, for a particular shade lasts but a moment, and once gone will not easily be discovered again. The crest of the hill at which I was now looking was full of wonderful colours the like of which were rarely to be seen in this region of Japan. Having taken the trouble to come here, I felt it a pity to waste this opportunity, and so decided to go and try my hand at reproducing these colours in a picture.

Sliding back the fusuma, I stepped out on to the verandah, and found O-Nami leaning against the shōji of the first-floor room opposite. Her chin was buried in the neck band of her kimono, so that only one side of her face was visible. I was on the point of calling out to her, when her left hand dropped to her side, and in the same instant her right hand moved like the wind. A flash, which might almost have been lightening, shot two or three times across her chest. Then came a sharp click, the flash vanished and in her left hand she was holding a white-wood sheath about a foot long. The next moment she disappeared behind the shōji. I left the hotel feeling that I had been watching a very early morning performance of Kabuki.[1]

I turned left out of the gate along a path which very soon began to slope gently upwards. Here and there I could hear the song of an uguisu. The ground to my right fell away into a peaceful valley which was one mass of mandarin orange trees, and to my left, two low hills stood side by side. Here too there seemed to be nothing but a profusion of orange trees. I had been to this area once some years before. I cannot be bothered to work out how many years ago that was, but anyway, it was in December, and it was cold. That was the first time I had ever witnessed the sight of a hillside completely covered with orange trees. I asked one of the pickers if she would sell me a few oranges, and she replied that I was welcome to as many as I wanted, free. Then, still perched at the top of a tree, she began to sing a strange melody. If this were Tokyo, I thought, I would even have to go and buy dried peel at a chemist's. In the evening, I heard guns being fired repeatedly, and when I asked what was happening, was told that it was the hunters out after wild duck. All this, of course, happened at a time

---

[1] Kabuki, like Noh, is a form of traditional Japanese drama.

when, as yet, I had been spared even so much as the sound of O-Nami's name.

O-Nami, I thought, would make a first class actress. When before the footlights, most actors and actresses have to assume a special manner for the occasion, but O-Nami was different: her home was her stage, and her life one continuous performance. She was, moreover, quite unaware that she was playing a part, for to act was second nature to her. Hers was what, I suppose, you might describe as an aesthetic life. Thanks to her, my study of art had been considerably advanced.

Her behaviour was such that, unless regarded as play-acting, it would seem weird, and rapidly become intolerable. Set against a background of stock concepts like duty and compassion, and viewed from the standpoint of the average novelist, it appears over-stimulated, and thus disagreeable. I could well imagine the probably unspeakable anguish which would result for me, an inhabitant of the world of reality, should any involved relationship develop between her and myself. Since the whole object of my present trip was to get away from everyday human ties, and do my utmost to become an artist, it was essential that I should regard everything I saw as a picture, and all the people I met as though they were merely performers in a Noh drama, or characters in a poem. Seen in the light of this resolution, O-Nami's behaviour and mode of life were more beautiful than those of any woman I had ever met. They were far more beautiful than those of an actress in a play, simply because she herself was not consciously trying to give a beautiful performance.

It would indeed be discourteous if people, misunderstanding these ideas, were to censure me as unfit to be a member of society. It is hard to follow the ways of virtue and righteousness, and the preservation of integrity is no easy task. Moreover, it requires courage to lay down one's life for honour's sake.

Since suffering awaits all those who dare these paths, there must be joy in the conquest of pain if we are to muster the necessary courage to do so. Painting, poetry and drama are but different names for this joy which is couched in misery. Only when we are able to appreciate the existence of such joy can our actions become heroic, our lives purged of impurity, and can we desire to gratify that supreme spark of poetry which lies within our hearts, by overcoming all hardship and privation. Only then are we able to disregard physical pain and material discomfort, and gladly suffer death at the stake in the cause of humanity. If it is possible to define art solely in the narrow terms of human emotion, then it is that uncompromising determination to forsake evil, and turn to virtue; to fight on the side of truth and justice in the war against iniquity; to help the weak and afflicted, and destroy the mighty, which has crystalized within the hearts of us men of culture, and which reflects the illuminating light of day.

A man whose behaviour is considered theatrical is laughed at. He is ridiculed if he should deviate so far from the human norm as to make an unnecessary sacrifice in order to convey the beauty of his feelings; and scoffed at for the absurdity of forcefully thrusting his views and ideas upon the world, instead of waiting for an opportunity to express his nobility of character by some natural means. It is permissible for those who really understand such things to laugh, but revilement by louts who have no capacity whatsoever for appreciating the finer feelings of others, and compare them with their own mean nature, is intolerable. There was once a young boy named Fujimura who commited suicide by plunging over a five hundred foot waterfall into the swirling rapids below. Before he died he wrote a poem called 'The Cliff-Top'.[1] As I see it, that youth gave

---

[1] Fujimura was one of Sōseki's pupils who in 1903 at the age of eighteen committed suicide by drowning himself.

his life—the life which should not be surrendered—for all that is implicit in the one word 'poetry'. Death itself is truly heroic. It is the motive which prompts it that is difficult to comprehend. What right, however, have those who are not even able to see the heroism of death to ridicule Fujimura's behaviour? It is my contention that they have no right at all, for being confined by their inability to sympathize with the concept of bringing life to a heroic conclusion, however much such a step may be justified by circumstances, they are inferior to him in character.

As an artist, my specialization in mood and sentiment raises me above my more prosaic neighbours, even though I am forced to share the same world with them. Furthermore, as a member of society, I occupy a position from which I may easily educate others, for I am more readily able to perform beautiful deeds than those who are strangers to poetry and painting, and have no artistic accomplishment. In our dealings with one another, a beautiful deed is virtue, justice and righteousness; and whoever manifests these in his daily life is a model to his fellow men.

I had, for a while, been able to stand aside and view the complexity of human emotions and relationships objectively, and there was no reason for me to become involved again, at least for the duration of this trip. In fact, it was imperative that I should not become involved, for if that should happen it would mean that all my efforts had been wasted. I had to take human nature, sift out the sand and grit, and then spend my time gazing at the beautiful gold which remained in the bottom of the sieve. I was not at present a member of society, but a pure artist who, having succeeded in severing the bonds of self-interest, was leading his life peacefully in a painted world. It goes without saying, of course, that it was essential for me to view the mountains, the sea and the people around me as no more than pieces of scenery, and to accept O-Nami's behaviour just as it was without question.

I had been following the path upwards for nearly a quarter of a mile, when I caught sight of the white wall of a building. Ah, a house among the orange groves, I thought. The path divided at this point, and I took the left-hand fork. As I did so, I looked back over my shoulder and saw a girl in a red skirt coming up from the valley. The red of her skirt gave way to the brown of her legs, which in turn ended at a pair of straw sandals. These sandals were gradually moving towards me. Wild cherry blossom was falling upon the girl's hair, and on her back she carried the sparkling sea.

The steep path eventually led me up to a plateau on a projecting spur of the mountain. To the north was a peak clothed in the green of spring. This was probably what I had seen from the verandah earlier in the morning. To the south was a strip of what I suppose would be termed burnt heathland. This was about sixty yards wide and terminated at the crumbling brink of a precipice. At the foot of the precipice were the two hills covered with orange trees which I had just passed, and looking out beyond the village, I saw, of course, the blue sea.

The path now split into many threads which converged and separated, crossed and recrossed in such a complex fashion that it was impossible to say that any of them was the main one. The result of this entanglement was that instead of every thread being a path, none of them was. The dark red earth of the tracks showed in irregular patches among the clumps of grass, and I found the unpredictability of its progress entertaining.

I wandered here and there through the grass looking for a suitable place to sit. The scenery, which when seen from the verandah had seemed a good subject for a picture, now appeared to be disappointingly unsettled. The colours too were slowly changing. Suddenly, while I was tramping back and forth across the plateau, the desire to paint deserted me. Since I was no longer seeking a vantage point, where I sat ceased to be of any importance; I could make myself comfortable anywhere. The spring sunshine penetrated to the very roots of the grass, and as I walked about wondering where to sit, I had the feeling that I was trampling unseen summer-colts underfoot.

Down there, the sparkling sea. The spring sunshine, unimpeded by so much as a flake of cloud, set the whole sheet of water aglitter, and its warmth was such that you could imagine it permeating right down to the sea-bed. The smooth surface of the sea was a study of torpid motion: one sweeping brush-stroke of dark blue, stippled with fine silver scales. The space beneath the heavens was filled with a limitless expanse of sparkling water on which the only discernible object was a white sail the size of a moth's wing. This, I thought, was how ships crossing with tributes from Korea must have looked in olden times. Apart from that sail, my whole world was sun and sea; the one giving light, and the other receiving it.

Flopping down on to the ground, I eased my hat up from my forehead so that it perched on the back of my head, and relaxed completely. Here and there the stunted forms of dwarf quince trees rose two or three feet out of the grass, and I now found myself face to face with one of them. The quince is an interesting tree. Its branches obstinately refuse to bend at all, and yet the overall effect is certainly not one of straightness. The whole lopsided framework of the tree is composed of short straight twigs and branches which collide with each other at an angle. The red or white blooms which appear in a rash over this framework look as though they do not know what they are doing there, and do not much care either. Even the soft leaves seem to have been stuck on at random. When you consider, the quince is the most foolish yet philosophical of all plants. There are people who are absolutely unconcerned with their inability to make any headway in the world, and make no effort to improve themselves. I am sure that they, in some future life, will be reborn as quince trees. I would very much like to be a quince myself.

Once, when I was a boy, I took a branch of quince, complete with blossoms and leaves, and amused myself by pruning it into a suitable shape for a writing-brush rack. When I had set my penny brushes so that their white spear-heads peeped out from among the blossoms and leaves, I placed the branch on my desk. That night when I went to bed, I thought of nothing but the quince brush-rack, and next morning, no sooner were my eyes open, than I leaped out of bed and ran to the desk to have a look at it. The flowers had died, and the leaves had shrivelled. Only the white brush-heads stood out as brightly as before. To me, it was inconceivable how such a thing of beauty could wither like that in one short night. Looking back on the incident, I realise that I was more unworldly then than I am now.

Here, up on the plateau, I had thrown myself down on to the ground, and had been greeted immediately by the quince, my old friend of twenty years ago. Staring at the flowers, I gradually started to drift, and a pleasant feeling stole over me. Once again I felt the inspiration to write, and lying in the grass, I began to arrange my ideas. I wrote down every line in my sketchbook as it came to me, and eventually when I felt I had done all I could, I read them through from the beginning.

My head was crammed with thoughts when I left home,
With spring's sweet breath playing around my skirts.

The rutted path is overgrown with fragrance,
And passes neglected into hazed obscurity.

Leaning upon my staff, I view each detail
Of bright Nature in her shining mantle.

A crystal cascade of nightingale's notes falls on the ear,
While air is filled with sweetest floral rain.

Beyond a wide and desolate plain I reach
An ancient temple, on whose door a poem I inscribe.

In uncompanioned loneliness I look towards the clouds
Where one wild goose, unskeined, wings homeward
    'cross the sky.

How deep, how recondite this seeming petty heart,
In whose recesses right and wrong lie dimmed by distance.

Although yet thirty, my thoughts are those of age,
But Spring retains her former glory.

Wandering here and there I am as one with everything in
    turn,
And 'midst the perfumed blossoms, peace is mine.

'Done it! I've done it!' The words escaped from me with a
contented sigh. This is what I had been waiting to write. These
lines exactly expressed my oblivion to the world while I had
been lying gazing at the quince blossoms. It did not matter that
there was no mention of the blossoms themselves, or of the sea;
it was enough that the poem expressed what I felt. I was happily
mumbling and muttering away to myself, when suddenly the
sound of somebody clearing their throat made me jump.

Rolling over on to my stomach, and looking towards where
the voice had sounded, I saw a man coming out from among
the trees which fringed the spur of the mountain. He wore a
battered brown Homburg, the brim of which was angled low
over his brow. I was unable to see his eyes, but I felt certain that
they were darting nervous glances from side to side. His dark
blue striped kimono tucked up around his loins, his bare legs

and wooden clogs told me very little about him, but his fierce unkempt beard gave him the air of a soldier of fortune.

Instead of descending the steep path which I had come up, as I expected him to do, the man stopped where it met the track he was on, turned and retraced his steps. I thought that he was going to disappear among the trees from whence he had originally emerged. But no, once again he turned and came back. Surely, I thought, only someone out for a stroll would walk to and fro across the heath like that, yet his whole attitude belied the idea. Moreover, I just could not imagine that such a person lived in this neighbourhood. From time to time the man would cock his head on one side, and then look all around him. He seemed to be lost in thought. He might, of course, be waiting for somebody; it was impossible to tell.

I eventually found that I was unable to take my eyes off this fearsome-looking character. I was not particularly scared of him, nor did I have any desire to paint him. However, I just could not tear my eyes away. I was swivelling my head from right to left, left to right, following his progress up and down when he finally came to a halt. No sooner had he done so than another figure appeared on the edge of my field of vision, and, as though in mutual recognition, the two gradually moved towards one another. The borders of my field of vision slowly began to close in, until at last they included no more than a tiny area right in the centre of the heath. The two figures now stood facing each other, almost touching. Behind one, were the mountains of spring, and behind the other, the sea.

One of the pair was, of course, the 'soldier of fortune'. And who was his companion? It was a woman—O-Nami! At the sight of O-Nami, I immediately recalled the dagger I had seen her with earlier that morning, and the thought that she probably had it concealed in her kimono sent a shiver of fear through me, even though I was supposed to be watching objectively.

For a while, the man and the woman remained perfectly still, both maintaining the same posture as when they had first come together. There was not a movement to be seen anywhere. They may perhaps have been talking, but I could hear nothing at all. The man at length allowed his head to slump forward on to his chest, and O-Nami turned away towards the mountains, so that her face was hidden from me. She appeared to be listening to an uguisu which was singing somewhere over there. A few moments later, the man drew himself upright and half turned on his heel. There was definitely something wrong. O-Nami spread her arms and silently swung round to face the sea. Something which looked like the hilt of a dagger was poking out from the top of her obi. Holding himself proudly erect the man started to move away. With just two steps, which her straw sandals rendered quite noiseless, O-Nami came up behind him. He stopped. Had she called out to him? He turned his head, and in that instant O-Nami's right hand dropped to her obi. *Look out*!

What flashed into view, however, was not the foot long dagger, but some kind of purse, the long drawstring of which swung back and forth in the spring breeze, as it dangled from the white hand extended to the man.

O-Nami stood with one foot advanced, and her body from the waist up leaning slightly backwards. On the outstretched palm of her white hand sat the purple-coloured purse. This posture alone was worth a canvas to itself.

The picture was interrupted by the dash of purple, but continued again after a space of two or three inches where the line of the man's half-turned body both complemented and qualified that of the woman in a superb fashion. I think that balance is the word that best describes the mood of that moment. Although in reality there was no contact between the two figures, for the purple purse sheered them off from one another, O-Nami seemed to be trying to pull the man to her, and he looked as though he were being drawn backwards. While they thus preserved the delicate harmony of their pose, it was born in upon me just how enormous was the contrast between their clothes, and between their faces. Having realised this, I regarded them as though they were part of a picture, and found them more fascinating than ever.

On one side a pair of thick bull-like shoulders surmounted by a black-bearded face; on the other the delicacy of an oval face with clear-cut features, above a swan neck and gracefully sloping shoulders. Here, the 'soldier of fortune' with his clumsily twisted body and wooden clogs; there, O-Nami managing to look elegant even in an everyday kimono, her dainty form curving gently backwards in a restrained arc. Added to this was the brown felt hat worn smooth with age, and the short, blue striped kimono of the man, set against the captivating femininity of O-Nami, whose well-combed hair so shone in the sunlight that the air about her head was set shimmering and dancing, and from whose black satin obi peeked the corner of a coloured under-sash. Viewed as a whole, the scene was a perfect subject for a picture.

The man put out his hand to accept the purse which was being offered to him, and as he did so the tableau, whose balance both had hitherto maintained by a skilful distribution of tension, crumbled. The woman was no longer pulling, and the man no longer being pulled. Although I am an artist, I had never realised that the state of mind of the models played so important a part in the construction of a picture. The couple separated, and moved off left and right. Now that they were devoid of any outward sign of feeling, it seemed incongruous to think of them as figures in a painting. The man paused and turned at the edge of the copse, but the woman continued walking without a backward glance. She was coming towards the place where I was lying, and soon was standing immediately in front of me.

'Sensei. Sensei,'[1] she called.

Oh Lord, that's done it, I thought, and wondered when she first realised that I was there.

'Yes, what do you want?' I asked, raising my head above the quince and losing my hat in the process.

'What on earth are you doing there?'

'I was lying down composing poetry.'

'Don't tell fibs. You were watching what happened just now, weren't you?'

'Just now? Just now, over there, you mean? Well, yes. I did just have a peep.'

'Ha, ha, ha, ha. You should have had a long look.'

'Well, to tell you the truth—I did.'

'There you are, you see! Oh please come out from among all that quince.'

I obeyed meekly.

'Was there something else you wanted to do among the trees?'

'No, I've quite finished thank you. I was just thinking of going home.'

'Then shall we walk back together?'

'All right.'

Once again I demonstrated my docility by going back in among the quince, gathering up my hat and painting materials, and then setting off side by side with O-Nami.

'Did you do any painting?'

'No, I gave up the idea.'

'You haven't painted a single picture since you came here, have you?'

'No.'

[1] Sensei literally means teacher, but may be used as a term of respect to anybody.

'But it's a waste isn't it, if having come here for the sole purpose of painting, you don't do any at all?'

'On the contrary, I make a profit whatever happens.'

'Oh, really? Why is that?'

'Because, when you come to work it out, the rate of interest is the same whether you paint a picture or not.'

'You and your puns. Ha, ha, ha, ha. You're a very happy-go-lucky person, aren't you. You take everything just as it comes.'

'If I didn't, it would mean I had wasted my time in coming to a place like this.'

'You should be happy-go-lucky wherever you are. If you're not, life isn't worth living. Take me for instance: I'm not at all ashamed that you were watching me just now.'

'You have no reason to be, have you?'

'Perhaps not. What do you think of that man I was with?'

'Well now, let me see. I'd say that whoever he was, he wasn't very rich.'

'Ha, ha, ha. You've hit the nail right on the head. You must be psychic. He came to get some money from me, because he says that he's so poor he cannot remain in Japan any longer.'

'Really? Where had he come from?'

'From down in the castle-town.'

'That's quite a way. And where is he off to?'

'It seems that he is set on going to Manchuria.'

'What for?'

'Who knows. To get some money maybe, or perhaps to die.'

As she said this, I raised my eyes and glanced at her face. Her mouth was set in a thin line, and the faint smile which usually hovered there was, for some unknown reason, beginning to fade.

'He is my husband.'

This statement, coming so unexpectedly, caught me completely off my guard, and I felt as though the woman had suddenly struck me. Naturally I had had no intention of getting such information out of her; nor had I had the slightest idea that she would confide in me to this extent.

'Well? What do you think of that? That surprised you, didn't it?' she asked.

'Yes, it did a little.'

'He isn't my husband now; we're divorced.'

'Oh, really. And. . .'

'That's all.'

'I see.—There's a beautiful white-walled house down there on the hillside, where all the orange trees are. It's nicely situated. Who does it belong to?'

'That's my elder brother's house. We'll drop in for a minute on the way home.'

'Is there something you want to do there?'

'Yes. I have to go there on an errand.'

'Very well then, let's go.'

We had arrived at the foot of the steep path, but instead of continuing down to the village, we turned sharply to the right and climbed upwards again for about a hundred and twenty yards until we came to a gateway. We went in, and waiving the formality of presenting ourselves at the front door, proceeded straight round to the entrance to the garden. O-Nami went in without the slightest hesitation, and so I followed suit. The garden which faced south, contained three or four hemppalms, and was bordered by a mud wall. Sloping away beyond this was an orange orchard. Sitting down on the edge of the verandah, O-Nami said, 'It's a lovely view. Look.'

'You're right, it is lovely.'

The room bordering the verandah was shut off by a line of shōji. I listened, but nothing stirred within. O-Nami showed no signs of announcing our arrival, but seemed quite content just to sit on the verandah and look at the orange orchard below. I thought this strange, and wondered what had brought her here in the first place. Finally all conversation lapsed, and we both sat looking down at the orange trees in silence. The sun, now nearing its zenith, shone full on the hillside, spreading its warm rays over the entire area, and penetrating to the depths of the foliage whose refurbished brilliance demanded attention. Presently there came the loud crowing of a cockerel from the direction of an outhouse.

'Good heavens! It's lunch time. I'd forgotten all about my errand.—Kyuichi, Kyuichi.'

O-Nami leaned backwards and slid open a shōji, revealing a room about fifteen feet by nine. This was empty save for two scroll paintings of the Kano school which hung, rather forlornly I thought, in a recess as an expression of the mood of spring.

'Kyuichi.'

At length an answering call came from the outhouse, followed by the sound of footsteps which eventually stopped on the other side of the fusuma across the room. Just as the fusuma was slid back, a white-wood sheath went rolling towards it across the matted floor.

'That's a farewell present from your uncle.'

I had not the faintest idea when O-Nami's hand had gone to her obi. All I saw was the dagger somersault two or three times in the air, then roll noiselessly across the matting to come to rest at Kyuichi's feet. Apparently the sheath was a loose fit, for as it lay there, I caught the glint of an inch of cold steel.

✦ 13 ✦

We went down to Yoshida by river-boat to see Kyuichi off at the station. Sitting in the boat were Kyuichi, old Mr Shioda, O-Nami, her brother, Gembei, who was taking care of the luggage, and myself. I, of course, had virtually just been asked along for the ride.

The fact that I had only been invited to make up the company did not stop me accepting, neither was I deterred by the fact that I could see no reason for my presence. For the duration of my 'non-human' trip, discretion was a word that was not in my vocabulary. The boat was flat-bottomed, and seemed to have been constructed by sticking sides on to a raft. The old man was in the middle, O-Nami and I were at the stern, Kyuichi and O-Nami's brother were in the bows, and Gembei sat by himself with the luggage.

'Kyuichi, do you like war, or not?' O-Nami asked.

'I won't know until I've had a taste of it. It will probably be pretty rough going at times, but I expect I'll enjoy myself sometimes too,' replied Kyuichi, who knew nothing at all about war.

'However hard it is, you must remember that it is for your country,' put in the old man.

'Doesn't it make you want to get in and fight somehow, having been given a dagger like that?' was O-Nami's next strange question.

'Yes, sort of.'

At this light response, the old man tugged at his beard and laughed, but his son sat there as though he had heard nothing.

O-Nami refused to be put off, and pushing her lovely face close to her cousin's, she continued, 'How can you fight if you're so indifferent?' Kyuichi exchanged a brief glance with the brother, then the latter turned and spoke to O-Nami for the first time.

'I'm sure you'll make a great fighter, O-Nami, if you ever become a soldier.' Judging from his tone, this was not said entirely as a joke.

'I? I become a soldier? I'd have become one long ago if I could, and I'd be dead by now. Kyuichi, you'd better die too. It's a disgrace to come out of a war alive.'

'Now, now, now. That's enough of such wild talk. Kyuichi, you must come marching home again in triumph. There are other ways to serve your country besides dying. I'm good for another two or three years myself yet. We'll be seeing each other again.'

As the thread of the old man's words spun out, it became thinner and weaker, until at last, no thicker than gossamer, it parted to spill the crystal beads of sorrow. He choked back his tears, thinking it shameful for a man to give way to his emotions before others. Kyuichi turned away without a word and looked towards the bank where, moored beneath a large willow tree, was a boat in which an angler sat gazing intently at his line. As we drew level, the wash from our boat rippled gently across the water. Looking up suddenly, the man caught Kyuichi's eye. Each sat there regarding the other steadily, but no spark of affinity passed between them. The man was thinking only of fish, but in Kyuichi's head there was not room for even a single carp. In uninterrupted calm, we moved on beyond the angler.

If you stood on the approach to the Nihonbashi bridge in

176

Tokyo, which hundreds of people cross every minute, and were able to elicit from each individual that went past what turmoil and confusion lay buried in his heart, you would find yourself bemused by the knowledge of what this world can do to a man, and life would become unbearable. There would have been no applicants for the job of standing at Nihonbashi and waving a flag to direct the trams were it not for the fact that the people a man in such a position meets come as strangers, and as strangers they go on their way. Fortunately, the angler did not ask Kyuichi for an explanation as to why he looked as though at any moment he was going to cry. Looking back, I saw that he was staring at his float contentedly. I expect he would have liked to sit there staring at it until the Russo-Japanese war was over.

The river was neither very wide nor very deep, and it flowed along at an easy pace. Wondering how long this smooth passage across the water with me leaning on the gunwale would continue, I realised that there would be no stopping until I reached a place where spring was no more, and where people were prepared to push and jostle one another aside in their frantic excitement. The young man, Kyuichi, on whose forehead Death had already made his putrid bloody mark, was dragging us all relentlessly along with him. The rope of Destiny was pulling him towards a distant, dark and grim land to the north, and so we too, who were inextricably bound to him by the circumstances of a certain day, month or year, would be drawn on until such time as the sequence of events set in motion by these circumstances should arrive at its inevitable conclusion. When that time came, there would a 'snip' between him and us, and he alone, with or without consent, would be reeled right up to Destiny's hand, while we would have no choice but to remain behind. No matter how much we might plead and struggle, we would be taken no farther.

I found the boat's smooth progress delightful. On either hand down by the water's edge were plants which I took to be horsetails, and along the top of the raised embankments were many willow trees, from among which at irregular intervals a low cottage showed its thatched roof and grimy windows. From time to time white ducks from the cottages would come quaking down the bank, and swim out into the river. The eye-catching points of brightness that stood out between the willows were presumably white peaches. I heard the repeated clatter of a loom at work, punctuated by the sound of a woman singing. The sporadic notes came echoing across the water, but it was impossible to tell what the song was.

'Sensei, will you do a portrait of me, please?' asked O-Nami. Kyuichi and O-Nami's brother were earnestly talking about the army, while the old man had dozed off at some time or other.

'Yes, all right,' I replied. Taking out my sketchbook, I wrote down the following lines.

Your obi has worked loose and flutters in the breeze,
But once again 'tis for pretence and not spring's passion
   it unwinds.
The maker's name, though woven in the silk,
Is, like your heart, unreadable.

When I showed this to O-Nami, she laughed and said, 'A quick sketch like this is no good. I want you to do a carefully detailed picture that expresses my character more.'

'I'd love to, but your face as it is at the moment wouldn't make a good picture.'

'What a charming compliment. Well, what do I have to do to make it a fit subject for a picture?'

'Now, calm down. I could paint it now really. But it's just that there's something missing, and I think it would be a pity to paint you without that something.'

'What do you mean, "something missing"? Since this is the face I was born with, there is nothing I can do about it, is there?'

'Even the face you were born with can be varied in many ways.'

'At will, you mean.'

'Yes.'

'That's right, make a fool of me because I'm a woman.'

'It's because you are a woman that you say such foolish things.'

'Well then, show me how you can make *your* face look different.'

'You've seen quite enough of the different ways my face can look.'

O-Nami fell silent, and turned her back on me. The embankments had disappeared, and now the ground on either side of the river was almost level with the surface of the water. This enabled me to see right across the neighbouring lowlands which were completely covered with wild milk-vetch in full bloom. The whole area was a sea of half-dissolved blossoms, as though the rain had at sometime caused the brilliant drops of scarlet colour to run. This sea stretched on and on to disappear eventually into the distant haze. Looking up I could see one huge precipitous peak towering into the sky, its upper part but dimly visible through a film of spring cloud.

'You climbed up the other side of that when you came to Nakoi,' said O-Nami, stretching her white hand out over the side of the boat, and pointing to the mountain about which there was an unreal, dream-like quality.

'Is the Tengu rock over there?'

'You see that splash of purple beneath the deep green?'

'You mean the shadow?'

'Shadow? It's a bare patch, isn't it?'

'No, it's a dip in the ground. If it were a bare patch it would look browner.'

'Maybe. Anyway, the Tengu rock is supposed to be just beyond that.'

'That would make the stretch of road with all the bends in it a little to the left.'

'No, that's a good way off. It's on the mountain behind that one.'

'Yes, that's right, it would be. At a guess I'd say it was about where that thin layer of clouds is.'

'Yes, somewhere near there.'

The old man, who had been dozing up till now, suddenly awoke with a start as his elbow slipped off the side of the boat.

'Aren't we there yet?' Pushing out his chest, he drew his right elbow back behind him, and thrust his left arm straight forward in a mighty fit of stretching and yawning which made him look for all the world as though he were practising archery. O-Nami burst out laughing.

'Sorry, it's a habit of mine. . . .'

'You look as though you like archery,' I remarked, joining in the laughter.

'In my younger days, I could draw a longbow that was an inch thick at the hand-grip. I can still give a better than average push with the left hand even now,' replied the old man patting his shoulder. In the bows, the discussion about war was at its height.

The countryside eventually gave way to more urban scenery, and our boat began to pass between houses. At one point a sign on the panel of a shōji announced that inside, savouries were served with the wine, and still farther on, we came to an old-fashioned tavern and a wood yard. Occasionally, we could even hear the sound of rickshaws. Above, swallows wheeled and twisted slowly in flight, and on the water ducks quacked. After a while, we left the boat and made our way to the station on foot.

I was being dragged back more and more into the world of reality. Anywhere that you can find a railway train must be classed as the world of reality, for there is nothing more typical of twentieth-century civilization. It is an unsympathetic and heartless contraption which rumbles along carrying hundreds of people crammed together in one box. It takes them all at a uniform speed to the same station, and then proceeds to lavish the benefits of steam upon every one of them without exception. People are said to board and travel by train, but I call it being loaded and transported. Nothing shows a greater contempt for individuality than the train. Modern civilization uses every possible means to develop individuality, and having done so, tries everything in its power to stamp it out. It allots a few square yards to each person, and tells him that he is free to lead his life as he pleases within that area. At the same time it erects railings around him, and threatens him with all sorts of dire consequences if he should dare to take but one step beyond their compass. It is only natural that the man who has freedom within the confines of his allocated plot, should desire to have freedom to do as he wishes outside it too. Civilization's pitiable subjects are forever snapping and snarling at imprisoning bars, for they have been made as fierce as tigers by the gift of liberty, but have been thrown into a cage to preserve universal peace. This, however, is not a true peace. It is the peace of the tiger in a menagerie who lies glowering at those who have come to look at him. If just one bar is ever taken out of the cage, the world will erupt into chaos, and a second French Revolution will ensue. Even now there are constant individual revolts. That great North-European writer, Ibsen, has cited in detail the circumstances which will lead to this outbreak. Whenever I see the violent way in which a train runs along, indiscriminately regarding all human beings as so much freight, I look at the individuals cooped up in the carriages, and at the iron monster itself which cares nothing at all for individuality, and I think, 'Look out, look out, or you'll find yourselves in trouble.' The railway train which blunders ahead blindly into the pitch darkness is one example of the very obvious dangers which abound in modern civilization.

We went and sat down in a tea-shop in front of the station. I stared at the rice-cake before me and thought about railway trains. This did not make me want to draw one, and there was no reason for me to impart my views to the others, so I ate my cake and drank my tea in silence.

Seated at the other table across the room were two men. They both wore identical straw sandals, but one was wrapped in a red blanket, while the other had on a pair of closely fitting light-green trousers which were patched at the knees. His hands resting on the patches completed the interesting contrast of colours.

'So it's no good after all then?' one of them was saying.

'No good at all.'

'It'd be all right if men had two stomachs like a cow. Then if anything went wrong with one of them, you'd just have to cut it out, and that'd be the end of the matter.'

Apparently, one of these countrymen was suffering from stomach trouble. They knew nothing of the stench which the wind was carrying across the plains of Manchuria, neither did they realise the shortcomings of modern civilization. As for revolution, why, they had never heard of the word. In all probability they were not even sure whether they had one or two stomachs. I took out my sketchbook and drew them.

Presently there came the shrill ringing of a bell, announcing the train's arrival.

'Well, shall we go?' suggested O-Nami standing up.

'All right,' agreed the old man also rising. Since we had already bought our tickets, we went straight to the barrier and passed through on to the platform. The bell continued to ring insistently.

There was a rumbling sound, and belching black smoke from its mouth, a serpent born of civilization came slithering its way over the silver rails.

'We'll have to say good-bye now,' said Mr Shioda.

'Yes. Well good-bye and take care of yourselves,' replied Kyuichi with a slight bow.

'Go and get killed,' said O-Nami for the second time.

'How about your luggage? Has it come? asked O-Nami's brother.

The serpent came to a halt in front of us, and as the many doors in its side opened, people began to stream in and out. Kyuichi climbed in, leaving the old man, O-Nami, her brother and myself standing on the platform.

One turn of the wheels, and Kyuichi would no longer belong to our world, but would already have gone to a world far, far away where men were moving midst the acrid fumes of burnt powder, and where they slipped and floundered wildly in a crimson quagmire, while overhead the sky was filled with the roar of unnatural thunder. Now he stood in the carriage about to depart for such a place, and stared at us mutely. This was where the rope of fate by which he had dragged us down from the mountains would be severed. The strands had, in fact, already begun to part. Although the carriage door and window stood open, although we could still see each other's face, and although there were no more than six feet between him who was to leave and us who were to remain behind, the rope was already fraying.

The guard ran along the platform towards us, slamming the doors as he came. With the closing of each door, the gulf widened between those that were leaving and those who had come to see them off. At length, Kyuichi's door banged shut, and the world was cut in half. Unconsciously the old man moved closer to the window, and Kyuichi put his head out.

'Look out there! She's off!' Before the last echoes of this cry had died away, there came the rhythmic blasts of steam being expelled from the engine as it slowly worked into its stride, and the train started to move. One by one the carriage windows passed by, and Kyuichi's face gradually grew smaller. As the last third-class carriage went past, another face emerged. There was the shaggy beard and well-worn brown Homburg of the 'soldier of fortune' who, filled with the sadness of parting, was taking one last look out of the window. Just then, he and O-Nami happened to catch sight of each other, but the engine continued to chug on, and very soon his face disappeared from view.

O-Nami gazed after the train abstractedly, but strangely enough the look of abstraction was suffused with that 'compassion' which had hitherto been lacking.

'That's it! That's it! Now that you can express that feeling, you are worth painting,' I whispered, patting her on the shoulder. It was at that very moment that the picture in my mind received its final touch.

1st September 1906